Praise for Miles In Time

"In Lee Matthew Goldberg's full-of-fun MILES IN TIME, fourteen-year-old Miles Hardy embarks on a time-traveling mission to save his brainiac brother's life. This madcap adventure finds Miles teaming up with his Past Self while trying to thwart an evil corporation from stealing the secret to his brother's time machine. You'll want to go back and read this again...and again...and again...for the very first time!"

Alan Orloff, author of the Anthony- and Agatha-Award winning YA thriller I PLAY ONE ON TV.

"Perfect for fans of Alex Rider, this time-travel mystery will have you flipping the pages to see what happens next. Readers will love wise-cracking Miles and his sidekick Kevin as they Sherlock in time, to find out who's after Miles' brother's time-travel invention. The best blend of mystery and adventure to keep even the most reluctant readers glued to the page."

Fleur Bradley, award-winning author of *MIDNIGHT AT THE BARCLAY HOTEL* and *DAYBREAK ON RAVEN ISLAND*

Praise for Runaway Train

"An engaging '90s pastiche with an earnest heart beating at its center."

"A mixtape of the 90s, paired with a beautiful story of love, loss, and finding yourself. I couldn't put it down!"

"Raw. Riveting…Realistic and shocking, hopeful and satisfying, Runaway Train will keep readers turning the page.

"Goldberg's storytelling is heartfelt, assured, and polished."

"All fans of '90s alternative, no matter their generation, will find something to love in this book. Runaway Train presents an adventure, an escape fantasy, and the possibilities of life when you're young and on the margins. This book is a delight for readers of all ages."

Alex DiFrancesco, author of *All City* and *Transmutation: Stories*

"Brimming over with the visceral atmosphere of the early 90s grunge era, Runaway Train is a must-read for those willing to buckle up for the ride."

Peter Malone Elliott, Book Pipeline

"A high-energy testimonial to the redemptive power of a road trip with an awesome sound-track. Lee Matthew Goldberg balances the urgency of youth with a whiff of anticipatory nostalgia for the music and misadventures of late adolescence."

Jenn Stroud Rossman, author of *The Place You're Supposed to Laugh*

TIME FIXERS

Also by Lee Matthew Goldberg

Runaway Train Series

Runaway Train

Grenade Bouquets

Vanish Me

Miles In Time Series

Miles in Time

TIME FIXERS

Miles In Time
Book 2

LEE MATTHEW GOLDBERG

WISE WOLF
BOOKS

"Time goes, you say? Ah, no! alas, time stays, we go."
Henry Austin Dobson

———

"Every new beginning comes from some other beginnings end."
Roman philosopher, Lucius Annaeas Seneca
"Closing Time" by Semisonic

TIME FIXERS

TIME FIXERS

Chapter One

I stood in the Jeremiah Boonton cafeteria eating my soggy lunch of chicken nuggets against a windowsill like I'd been forced to do for the entire school year. I was supposed to meet my best friend Kevin so we could hunt for a seat together, but he'd probably fallen asleep in his pre-algebra class again and no one bothered to wake him up. Like always, the cafeteria was divided between the jocks and cheerleaders, the Brainiacs, and the alternative burnouts, none of which had any desire to include me at their tables. Ninth grade was winding down, but Kevin and I were still as invisible as ever.

If only all of them knew what I'd been able to accomplish this year, I thought, imagining that I'd be an instant celebrity if everyone at school found out that I'd freaking traveled back in time!

Just months ago, I discovered that my genius brother Simon had been killed over his mechanical glove time machine. But before he was killed, he left me a message to use his time machine to travel a week into the past to solve his murder. Being a budding detective, this had been the kind of BIG CASE I'd always been waiting for, and I was able to prevent him from dying. Now I'd been back in my sleepy Iowa hometown for months, and my time traveling adventure was starting to feel like a dream.

"Miles," Kevin said, huffing and puffing over while holding a tray overflowing with mushy nuggets swimming in ketchup. "Sorry I—"

"Fell asleep in class, I know."

I moved my tray to make room for Kevin's on the windowsill.

"How did you know I fell asleep?" Kevin said, blinking the crust out of his eyes. His curly red hair was flat on one side and in shock mode on the other, probably from using his desk as a pillow.

"Because you have pre-alg before lunch on Wednesdays and you always fall asleep during pre-alg."

Kevin swiped a mushy nugget and popped it in his mouth.

"Oh yeah, you're right." He shrugged. "I guess I do."

"You always say that as a response, too," I said, feeling more bored than ever on this particular day. I longed to put on the mechanical glove that Simon had created to transport me anywhere but Frontier.

"Any cases come up lately for *Mr. Hardy's Detective Agency*?" Kevin asked, stuffing two more nuggets into his mouth before he finished the one that was already there.

We had started our detective business out of Kevin's tree house back in elementary school. I was the president and recently made Kevin a VP after years as my lowly assistant. Ever since we saved Simon, Kevin

2

had wanted to become a more integral part of the agency, but unfortunately there were no other BIG CASES to solve. Our last measly one involved getting paid in pies like usual to find Ms. Kissey's cat Peaches, who ran away again from the old nagging woman.

"I checked our website this morning and…nothing." I pouted, nibbling on a gross nugget that had the consistency of a wet tissue.

Kevin took a long sip of his strawberry milk. "I'm sure something will come up soon."

Something had, in fact, come up about a month ago. Simon came home one day completely on edge. He'd noticed someone following him who fit the description of the people from Omni, the evil corporation who tried to kill him in the first place. More importantly, he'd also sent his guinea pig Stinkers a year into the past. Previously, I'd only been able to travel back to when Simon created the time machine, but now that Stinkers had returned from that far in the past, it meant we could travel to any era.

We had decided on 1999 so we could stop our grandfather from losing his job. He'd become bitter and abused his wife Lillian, who in turn, abused my mom and made her into the pill-popping zombie she was today. Mom's only chance at having a normal life would be if Simon and I were able to rewrite the unfortunate past she'd been born into.

But Simon said the time machine wasn't ready for a trip like that…yet. While Stinkers had traveled a year into the past and survived, Simon wanted to be absolutely certain that we could go back almost twenty-five years without endangering ourselves. He had created a special collar for Stinkers that linked with the mechanical glove and allowed Stinkers to return to the present after a certain set time; but there was no telling if it would work with someone bigger than a pound or two. Simon still wanted to tinker with it more while I was ready to just take a chance and go, go, go!

The bell rang as students began packing up their knapsacks and zooming to the exit.

"Oh no," Kevin said, stuffing all the remaining nuggets into his mouth until it looked as if he was hoarding tennis balls in his cheeks. He stuck a straw between his lips and attempted to wash down the food with some strawberry milk; but it all became too much to hold in and he spit out the half-chewed grub onto his tray.

"Dude," I said. "We're gonna be tenth graders soon. If you ever want to get a girl to give you a second glance, you can't keep behaving like an animal."

Kevin spit one last nugget onto his tray and murmured a halfhearted, "Sorry. Won't do it again."

"C'mon," I said, dumping Kevin's regurgitated food into the garbage.

As we fell into the crowd pushing toward the cafeteria's doors, I pictured this same scenario happening next week, and again, and again until the weeks in a sleepy town like Frontier all blurred into one another.

That would be my future...unless I heard from Simon that we were finally ready to head back to the past.

I closed my eyes and pictured getting this awesome news when I got home. Hopefully, the thought of it might be enough to get me through the rest of the crappy school day.

Chapter Two

I dashed up to Simon's room once I got home from school. Something told me that today was going to be the day he'd be ready to go back in time. I imagined putting on the mechanical glove Simon used for his time machine and soaring through the lightning tunnel like I had months ago. Seeing all the stars and galaxies rushing by had been awe-inspiring, but this time it'd be with my brother at my side on a mission to save our mom. The thought made me giddy.

Simon had removed the DON'T ENTER sign off his door a while back, but it didn't matter since the door was locked and no one was answering. When he felt like he was being followed, he installed extra locks for his room just in case someone tried to kill him... again. I didn't think it necessary since he was never at home anyway.

Simon had set up shop in a new lab while he worked on any last-minute tweaks for the time machine. Even though Smith Sumpter, the man who tried to kill him, sat in jail, Simon figured that Omni had found out about his lab in the barn off Generator Street. So he and his physics teacher Elton Congley gutted the lab and moved it all somewhere else. He hadn't told me the location yet, worrying that the information could harm me if Omni came looking. The new lab would be revealed once the time machine was completely ready.

It was almost four o' clock, which meant that I had a date with Maisie, my new long-distance gf. After the whole fiasco with her father Smith trying to kill Simon, her grandparents took her to Chicago and enrolled her in The Arts Academy School. While I hadn't physically seen her since she left over six months ago, the two of us tried to talk in some form every day. She always had a million stories about all of the amazing new friends she made at art school with names like Slade and Agatha, or the amazing instructors who inspired her, or the *amazing* exhibit she saw at the Art Institute of Chicago. I hated to be jealous, but I couldn't help it. I never had anything *amazing* to tell her since Simon warned me not to discuss the time machine with ANYONE ELSE, even her.

Maisie had invited me to a Life Drawing art show she was putting on in Lincoln Park with other students this coming weekend, but my dad wouldn't let me go to Chicago on my own. He had promised that we'd go to see her in Chicago eventually, but he'd been so consumed with helping Mom lately that he didn't have time to be bothered with anything else.

Over the past few weeks, Mom had gotten worse than she'd ever been. I would wake up in the middle of the night to hear her howling like a dog while Dad attempted to calm her down. She had started pulling out her hair as well. Once long and luscious, her dark hair now had bald patches. She even picked at her eyebrows and eyelashes and was beginning to resemble an alien, wandering around the house with a flannel blanket wrapped around her body, mumbling about going "home." She refused to listen that she was already there.

Down the hall, I could hear yelling coming from my parents' bedroom now and Mom howling about "going home" again. I was about to ignore it and head to my room to call Maisie when the sound of someone hurtling themselves into a door shook the hallway. My stomach lurched at the thought of Mom bashing her head and bleeding so I ran to their bedroom and flung open the door to find Mom curled up on the floor. She wasn't bleeding, but she was rubbing her arm and crying softly. Dad sat on the bed with his face in his hands. When he raised his head, he looked like an old man. What little hair he had left started graying over the last few months.

"I'm just lost, Miles," he confessed. "I don't know what else to do."

"What happened?"

We both glanced at Mom, who sat up against the wall hugging her knees.

"I've made a decision," Dad said, taking off his glasses to rub his tired eyes. "A few weeks ago, I told your mom that I'll be putting her in a home."

This recent development must've been why Mom had been wandering around the house muttering about "going home."

"Just for a trial period, a week at most to see how she does."

Mom tilted her head back and let out a howl that could rival any wolf's.

"What's the place?"

Dad's knees cracked as he rose. He went over to the dresser and brought back a brochure. The Piece of Mind Center. The front cover had a cartoon patient with an enlarged brain in the shape of a pie and one slice missing. A smiling doctor was reinserting that missing piece. Their tagline was, "Feel Full Again."

"When does she go?" I asked, handing back the brochure.

Mom let out another howl, louder than before.

"Come," Dad said, and led me into the hallway. He closed the bedroom door behind him.

"What if she tries to hurt herself again while the door's closed?" I asked.

Dad fiddled with his glasses and gave a slight smile. "I have some news, Miles. I might have an investor."

We heard knocking coming from inside the bedroom, softly at first until the knocks became more impatient.

"Goddammit, Patricia, can you give me a minute?" Dad yelled, knocking back. "Just a *minute* is all I ask. Please."

The knocks softened, but didn't stop completely.

"What investor are you talking about, Dad?"

"For the UniZoom! My motorized unicycles." Dad let out a wide grin and then frowned, as if he realized he shouldn't be happy at this moment. "This bigshot in Chicago is very interested. He's willing to give me thousands if the prototype is up to snuff. I have to go to Chicago this weekend to see him."

Upon hearing Dad mention Chicago, the butterflies in my stomach started flapping their wings because Maisie's art show was happening there this weekend too. I imagined how great it would be to see her drawings and snag a kiss. But then I felt guilty, since I should be worrying about Mom rather than how I could score.

"The Piece of Mind Center is in Farley on the way to Chicago. I wanted to drop your mom off on my way. This place can really help. And then we can make a definite decision about what is best for her."

I thought about living with Mom these last few years. Feeding her pill after pill. Combing the knots out of her hair. Brushing her teeth as if she was an invalid. I choked on the tears building up in my throat.

"C'mere, son," Dad said, with his arm around my shoulder. Dad wasn't much for hugs, so it felt good to be nuzzled into his armpit for once. He was crying too, but I could tell that he didn't want me to see.

"It's okay, Dad. I know you've done everything you can."

"I want you to come with us. I'd ask Simon to come as well if I ever knew where the hell that kid was. Anyway, I know it'd make it easier for your mom if you were there."

"Of course, I'll go," I said, and then since Dad hadn't brought it up, I decided to ask: "My girlfriend Maisie is having an art show in Chicago this weekend. Would I be able to go while you're meeting with the UniZoom investor?"

Dad stopped hugging me, and instantly I missed his comforting touch. I was afraid he would be angry for having such a selfish son while Mom was going through such a difficult time.

"Girlfriends…" Dad sniffled. "Next thing I know you'll be on your own far away from here."

"I still got all of high school left."

"Of course, you can see your girlfriend's art show. This family has to start living as much as possible, despite your mom's ailment. She'd hate be a determent to your happiness, I know that would hurt her the most."

"Do you think she'll ever come home?" I asked, as I heard her soft howls of "home, home" slipping through the crack under the door.

"Yes, I do, son. We'll get her back someday. Okay?"

Dad took a deep breath as he put his hand on the doorknob to the bedroom.

"Now run along and go tell your girlfriend you'll be seeing her soon in Chicago."

"I will. Thanks, Dad."

The bedroom door opened as Dad stepped inside. Mom was looking at both of us in disgust, as if she knew we were trying to get rid of her.

"I love you," I mouthed to her, but she growled back in response as Dad closed the door.

Even though I had a Snap date with Maisie later and good news to tell her about coming to Chicago to see her art show, I didn't have it in me to talk to her face-to-face. I was worrying too much about what it'd be like to drive up to the Piece of Mind Center and watch as Mom got dragged away.

So I just sent Maisie a simple text that said,

> Goin 2 yer art show this wknd. Will
> explain more when i c u.

I debated whether to end the text with a smiley face, which was how we often ended our texts to each other, but I didn't feel like smiling at that moment so I just hit send.

Chapter Three

Dad turned up the radio on the drive to Farley since Mom wouldn't stop howling. We had buckled her in the back seat, but she was thrashing around so much that we had to stop the car somewhere along the border of Iowa and Illinois so I could sit in the back seat to calm her down. As we got back on the road, the radio played Y2K pop music from my parents' high school years. N'SYNC's "Bye Bye Bye." "(You Drive Me) Crazy" by Britney Spears, and Len's "Steal My Sunshine." The songs seemed to mirror how I was feeling about shuttling Mom off to the Piece of Mind Center.

For the entire drive, Dad and I stayed quiet, both of us probably feeling guilty about using this trip to the institution for our own personal gain. When we reached Farley, Mom seemed to know that something was up. She quit howling and had now taken to chewing her tongue instead. Droplets of blood dribbled down her chin.

"Maybe this was a bad idea," I said. I wanted to

tell Dad to wait a little longer so Simon and I could travel to 1999 and try to fix Mom's family, but echoes of Simon's warning that NO ONE can know about the time machine caused me to keep my big mouth shut.

My stomach turned as we reached the Piece of Mind Center. It was the only building in the middle of nowhere, surrounded by a lot of trees. A nurse waddled outside with a clipboard and a frozen smile.

"Howdy doo," she gushed as Dad and I got out of the car.

Dad signed all the paperwork and the nurse bounced on her heels. I guessed that this place probably thought giddiness was the best way to combat mental illness.

"Yoo hoo, Patricia," the nurse cooed as she leaned into the back seat.

Mom sat still, no more howling, no more thrashing around. I wondered if she had given up.

The nurse unbuckled Mom's seat belt and Mom's eyes shot open. She went right for the nurse's cheek and dug her teeth in. The nurse let out a cry as other attendees in white coats rushed for the car. Mom and the nurse tumbled out of the back seat. There was blood on the asphalt, but I didn't know if it was from Mom chewing her tongue or because she bit the nurse's cheek. Two attendees restrained Mom and stuck a needle in her arm as the nurse scurried away in tears.

"This is where she needs to be…for now," Dad said, squeezing my shoulder hard enough for it to hurt.

I watched the attendees take Mom away as Lenny Kravitz's "Fly Away" blared from the car. That was exactly what I wanted to do. Fly away from my life at that moment, from Mom's sad stare. Now that the drugs had kicked in, she seemed so hopeless, so lost, a string of drool running from her bloody lips. I yelled at the white coats to wipe the drool away, to keep her presentable. One of them listened and ran a handkerchief across her mouth as the electric doors opened and Mom was dragged inside.

Dad took his hand off my shoulder and got back in the car. He turned off the radio, but the silence was worse. I kept watching the entrance as if Mom might emerge, free from her sick mind, human again. She never appeared. I tucked my chin into my chest and lumbered for the car, sliding in next to Dad as the motor idled before we shot out of the parking lot.

As the trees flew by, I swore that when I returned from Chicago, I'd convince Simon that we had to go to 1999 no matter what, otherwise we'd better get used to the Piece of Mind Center becoming Mom's home.

I knew once someone entered a place like that, they rarely ever came back out.

Chapter Four

Dad dropped me off at Maisie's art show and I tried not to worry about Mom for the time being. Soon enough, Simon and I would be traveling to 1999 and the reality of her being mentally unstable could be changed. Hopefully, it would become nothing more than a forgotten nightmare.

During the entire trip from Farley, Dad went over his pitch to the UniZoom investor. He wanted to market it to some hipster kids in their early twenties who'd think that a motorized unicycle was an ironic way to get around. I had suggested marketing it to kids my own age since someone in their twenties could just get a car instead—but Dad didn't want to hear it.

Neither of us brought up Mom during the ride and I was glad for that. As I got out of the car, I thought Dad might try to have a heart-to-heart, but when he leaned from the car window all he said was. "Gotta zoom, Miles. Time's a wastin'."

I headed down the block to the art show and saw a girl with bright pink hair and thick glasses without lenses checking names at the door. For a second, I got nervous that my name wouldn't be on the list since I told Maisie I was coming last minute, but then the girl waved me inside with her pretty pink fingernails.

I entered a sleek space with flashing lights and electronic beats pumping from overhead speakers. The place was packed with artsy types: men with goatees and berets, stick-thin women dressed in black, and grungy kids my age with uncomfortable-looking piercings. They all were commenting on the paintings and drawings of nude people covering the walls. I couldn't believe that everyone else could keep a straight face without pointing and cracking jokes. One painting I saw was of a woman with boobs for eyes and a smile instead of a belly button. I imagined Kevin would be laughing hysterically if he were here.

Even though I tried, I couldn't stop thinking about Mom being dragged away to the Piece of Mind Center earlier. At least she'd be better off there until Simon and I were able to travel back. This way we wouldn't have to worry about administering her pills or whether she was chewing her tongue off. I winced at the thought of her clamping down on the nurse's cheek and spitting a chunk of her flesh into the air.

"Miles?" I heard a sweet voice say from behind and turned around to see Maisie. I'd been so nervous if things between us would be like it was when she left Frontier. Six months was a long time to be apart in a relationship, especially since this was the *first* relationship I'd ever been in, and I had no idea what I was doing.

"Hey, Maisie!"

I put on a goofy grin and then got worried about acting too excited to see her. The other day I'd overheard some seniors saying that girls liked when guys played hard to get, but I'd been picturing this awesome reunion with Maisie for months and I was never a good actor anyway.

We both leaned in for a herky-jerky hug. I moved to the left. She did the same. I moved to the right and she did as well. Finally, I stuck out my hand for her to shake and she laughed.

"Stay still," she said, and left a kiss on my cheek that I could feel all the way down to my toes. "You look taller."

I blushed. She was the most amazing thing I'd seen since I watched her drive away from Frontier half a year ago. She had added a streak of royal blue to her blonde hair and was wearing makeup. She wiped the lipstick kiss off of my cheek.

"Thanks," I said. I could feel my cheeks burning and wished I could just calm down.

"This is so cool that you came! My grandparents aren't into art, so it's nice to have someone see my work besides other students and my teachers."

"Yeah, wow, this is so exciting," I said, looking around at the crowd that had become bigger and bigger since I entered. The space was almost filled to capacity.

"A.A. goes all out for our final projects of the year. That's what we call Arts Academy. Kind of an inside joke. Since the school's so cutthroat, it could turn anyone into an alcoholic."

A boy and a girl slinked up behind Maisie. The boy was thin and wore what looked like a skirt. He had black hair with a green stripe that swooped across his eyes and a pocketbook big enough to fit a bowling ball. The girl had shaved her head but tattooed a streak of red across her scalp. She had about two dozen piercings between her nose, lips, and ears.

"Oh Miles, this is Slade and Agatha," Maisie said, as I held out my hand for them to shake. Slade and Agatha scowled back.

"We don't shake hands," Agatha said, with her pierced nose in the air. I wondered how awful it must be for her when she had a cold.

"Yes, our hands are our most cherished assets and we never take the risk of exposing them," Slade added.

They both raised their hands to show they were wearing gloves.

"Oh sure, yeah that makes sense," I said, trying to be nice in front of Maisie even though her new friends were clearly asswipes.

"Miles came to visit me from Iowa where I used to live," Maisie said as Slade and Agatha snickered.

"Iowa," Slade mumbled under his breath. "Land of cornfields and not much else."

I was about to shove Slade to the ground for an obnoxious comment like that, but then I figured defending Iowa wasn't worth upsetting Maisie.

"No, I liked Iowa," Maisie said. "The sunsets there, it's not the same in Chicago. Sometimes it would get so quiet that you can hear yourself think and really get inspired."

"So, what's your analysis of all our works?" Agatha asked me, fiddling with one of her lip rings that had a skull on it.

"I don't know much about art," I admitted as my palms got sweaty. I hated to be put on the spot about any subject but history, but then I saw Slade and Agatha rolling their eyes, so I figured I needed to say something.

"Some of the paintings look so real." I nodded toward a painting of an elderly woman sitting on a stool and covering up her unmentionables with a large bowl of well-placed fruit. "Except for that one," I continued, pointing at the drawing I'd seen earlier with boobs for eyes and a smile in place of a belly button. "That one is just weird. I'd like to have some of what that artist was smoking when they drew that."

Maisie looped the blue streak of hair around her ear and gazed at the floor.

"That one's mine," she mumbled so softly, that for a second, I didn't know whether or not she'd actually spoken.

"Oh my god...delicious," Slade chimed in as he and Agatha gave each other a high-five. "You just got burned, sister." He jabbed a finger in Maisie's face.

"No...I mean, it's cool that it's weird," I stammered as the room started to spin. I couldn't believe my big dumb mouth. "I like weird things...really. I mean...I noticed that drawing before any of the others, and I'll honestly remember it more than all the rest."

"You don't have to say that," Maisie mumbled again.

"No, I mean it. Really. Like...it's innovative."

"Or derivative," Agatha said. "Picasso was into moving around body parts a hundred years ago."

Maisie looped the strand of blue hair around her ear again, finding solace in the repeated action.

"Maybe you're the derivative one," I said, not quite knowing what that meant. "Like you think all of your piercings are so cool and it makes you *so* different than everyone else, but what happens when you sneeze, huh? I bet your snot always leaks out of the tiny holes and—"

"You really know how to pick 'em, Maisie," Agatha said, taking Slade by the arm. "We're going to mingle with art aficionados who actually know what they are talking about."

"Hmrph," Slade said, slinging his giant pocketbook over his shoulder and marching away with Agatha.

"I'm sorry," I said. "I didn't mean to say that to her. It's been a long day."

The last few minutes had been the first time I'd forgotten about Mom since I learned about the Piece of Mind Center.

"Look at everyone crowded around Slade and Agatha's work," Maisie said. The tone of her voice didn't convey jealousy, just sadness. I felt bad that no one seemed to be paying much attention to her wild drawing.

"You know what's lame?" I said as Maisie looked up through the beginnings of tears. "Being appreciated in your time as an artist. I bet in the future your work is gonna make millions and no one will know who those two are."

"That's unlikely," she said, looking down at her hands as if she was angry with them for not being able to create the kind of genius she had hoped.

"Right now is just a moment in time, nothing more. There will be other art shows, and—"

"Do you want to get out of here?" Maisie asked.

"Sure, whatever you want to do. I mean…we can stay if you want. I feel like such a boob for what I said earlier." He slapped his forehead. "I'm sorry, I didn't mean to say boob again."

"My drawing was a comment on how women are

treated in society. Men look at us and all they see are breasts."

She'd been hugging her arms close to her chest, but when she removed them, I could see how much she had changed since I saw her last.

I bit my lip to avoid saying anything like a stereotypical guy.

"C'mon," Maisie said, taking my hand. Hers was warm but not clammy. She had been drawing earlier and left charcoal stains on my palm.

We weaved through the burgeoning crowd until we were outside, and Maisie started to cry with silent tears that dripped down her freckled cheeks. I wanted to hug her, but I was afraid she'd push me away. So I stood there twiddling my thumbs while she wiped her eyes with her long sleeves.

"I want Franks N' Dawgs," Maisie decided, heading into a restaurant down the block without turning around to see if I was following.

And of course, I followed. I knew that I always would.

Chapter Five

At Franks N' Dawgs, Maisie tore into an epic Porkgasm hot dog with bacon sausage, bacon jam, whiskey-glazed pork belly, Baconnaise and ham dust. I felt weird for ordering a plain dog with just ketchup and mustard. Even the guy at the counter looked at me funny and tried to talk me into one of their more out-there concoctions.

"I hate it here," she said with pork belly hanging from her mouth.

"We could've eaten somewhere else—"

"No, I mean I hate it here in Chicago with my grandparents, A.A., and pretentious people like Slade and Agatha."

"You always made it sound like this was such a great experience."

"What other choice do I have? I'm stuck here. My dad's in prison, my mom has vanished."

The hot dog she was eating slid out of its bun and landed on the floor. This seemed to set her off even more.

"Can nothing go right?"

She tossed the remaining food onto her plate and put her head in her hands.

"Look, I'm pretty miserable back in Frontier, too," I said, but she still kept her head in her hands. "My detective agency has gotten no new cases and my mom…"

My voice cracked when I mentioned Mom. Finally, Maisie raised her head.

"What about your mom?"

"Let's just say she's out of the picture for now, too."

"But you still have your dad and your brother and friends like Kevin. Miles, I have no one."

"You have me."

A smile curled on the left side of her face.

"But you're about to head back to Iowa and then I'll have to face Slade, Agatha, and all the rest of them while they make fun of my work. Even the teachers at A.A. are cruel. One of them told me I'd never make enough money from my art to even cover my rent." She picked at a wilted piece of bacon on her plate. "God, I wish I could just take off somewhere for a while."

"Where would you go?"

"Anywhere but here. Somewhere far, far away from my grandparents. All they talk about is how much I look like my mom. We have the same hair, same expressions, it's like they don't even know how much it hurts to hear them talk about her."

Right before Maisie left for Chicago, she told me that her mom's name was Talia. I had overheard her dad Smith say that Omni had sent someone named Talia back in time two years ago, but she never wound up returning. I almost told Maisie back then about her mom, but I knew she wouldn't understand. To her, time travel only existed in far-fetched movies.

"I've been waiting to go far, far away, too," I said. Once the words left my mouth, I couldn't believe I'd been so careless. But part of me wanted to confess to her everything about the time machine: saving Simon's life, her dad's involvement with Omni, the reason her mom disappeared. It was killing me to keep it all bottled up.

"Well, if you could go anywhere where would you go?"

"1999," I said, playing along, trying to be comical. I watched her expression change. I wondered if her mom had looked at Smith the same way when he told her she'd be traveling back in time. Maisie's face radiated absolute awe.

"I love that era," she gushed. "Pre-9/11, everything seemed so happy. Pop music like Britney Spears and the Backstreet Boys, like it was so unironically fun. The art was like that too. Jeff Koons and his giant balloon sculptures. Stuckism that valued painting as a medium, its use for communication and the expression of emotion and experience. The opposite of Slade and Agatha that are going for nihilism and irony of conceptual art."

Her tears had completely dried up and she was smiling bigger than I'd ever seen her smile before. Her eyes glazed over and I knew she was picturing herself in 1999. I wanted to tell her that I could make it possible. That I'd take her there so she could smile like this forever. I guessed that sometimes she probably went home and cried herself to sleep from all the terrible things that had happened to her.

"Just a dream, right?" She winked, and the smile was gone. The sad girl had returned.

"Maybe not," I said, and leaned in close so no one else could hear what I was about to say.

She looked at me funny. This conversation was definitely taking a strange turn.

"I'm going to tell you something," I said. Even though Simon had warned me not to say anything to anyone about the time machine, I was tired of keeping it a secret from Maisie. She deserved to travel back with us since her life in the present had been so tough these past couple of years. Maybe after we'd prevent my grandfather from losing his company, we could try to find out where her mom might be.

"You need to promise me that you'll stay calm when I tell you this," I added.

She tucked her hands in her sleeves.

"You're freaking me out, Miles."

"No, this isn't a bad thing. It's a very good thing. But this will need to stay between us. No one else can know."

"Okay."

So I told her…almost everything. I decided to leave out the part about her mom for now since it was so much information at once. I started with Simon creating the time machine and our mission to go back to 1999. Then I confessed about traveling back a week to save Simon from being murdered. I was about to explain how Smith was involved, but she had already made the connection.

"That's why my dad wanted your brother dead?"

All the information was still too much for her to handle. She rubbed her forehead, as if in pain.

"Your dad works for this company call ChronOm-niclast, or Omni for short. They want Simon's time machine for their own purposes."

She started crying and I found myself tearing up as well. She wiped her face, but the tears kept coming.

"My dad wanted to see me after he was sent to prison," she said, shaking her head. "But I refused. I didn't...I'm trying to keep a certain memory of him, not of him as a killer."

"But that's what he is."

"I know that!" She took a deep breath. "I'm sorry...it's just, that's my dad, you know? I realize who he actually is, but to me, he was...perfect."

"Come with us," I said, taking her hands in mine.

"Come with you where?"

"To 1999. Simon is finishing up the final tests, we're almost ready to go."

"I'm in school..."

"But if you're not happy here? You can help us with our mission and then we could—"

I was about to mention her mom. The truth hung from my tongue, but I kept quiet. It'd be cruel to tell her news like that unless we really had a plan to find her. As of now, her mom could be lost in any era.

"That way we could spend more time together." I shrugged. "You won't have to worry about dealing with your grandparents or all of the pretentious d-bags at your school."

"Time travel..." she said as if the thought just occurred to her. "And it really works?"

I looked around to see if anyone was watching us. Everyone seemed to be concentrating on their hot dogs.

"You go through this lightning tunnel. It's wild. And then all of sudden you're yanked back in time."

Now Maisie was looking around the restaurant, getting nervous.

"You realize that this discovery changes the world."

"Simon wants to keep it under wraps. We'll go back in time to change my family's history so my mom has a chance at a normal life, but that's it for right now."

"These people my dad works for, they weren't arrested with him. They must be after Simon—"

"I'm guessing that they've been rebuilding their operation. But yes, we haven't seen the last of them. It's obviously dangerous to get involved with this, but—"

"I'll do it," she whispered, and then the left side of her mouth curled into a smile. "I'll definitely do it. When do we go?"

"Like I said, Simon's doing some final tests but very soon…"

I stopped talking because something had shifted her concentration. She was staring at the door to Franks N' Dawgs.

"Maisie, what is it?"

"This older lady, I don't know, it just looked like she was watching us."

"Which older lady?"

"She just left. I saw her staring right at us. It seemed like she was trying to hear what we were saying."

"C'mon," I said, grabbing her sleeve and yanking her out of the restaurant. Outside we looked down the block, but didn't see any older woman.

"How old was the woman?" I asked, breaking a sweat, my heartbeat accelerating.

"Old but not that old."

"What did she look like?"

I was scared, but didn't want to freak Maisie out. She was freaked out anyway.

"She had…I dunno…short hair, silver hair, I guess. Kinda spikey."

I remembered being at Omni's headquarters with my past self before Smith deployed the bomb that blew it all up. A spikey-haired older lady had been the one who noticed us. She had tiny eyes and a skeletal face. Weeks later Simon said that he noticed a lady with a similar description following him. It had to be the same woman.

"Miles, what is it?"

"I think I'm being watched. I think you are now, as well."

A car pulled up in front of us. The driver leaned hard on the horn, tapping it a few times. We jumped at the noise.

"Who's that?" Maisie yelped, clamping her hands over her mouth.

I looked closer and saw that it was Dad who had come to pick me up. The window rolled down and Dad stuck his head out.

"Time to go, Miles."

He didn't look pleased.

"I shouldn't have told you anything," I said to Maisie, giving her a hug as I whispered into her ear. "I don't want you to be in danger."

Her heart was beating against my chest. The adrenaline rushing between the two of us had reached a full tilt.

"No, I'm glad you told me. I…"

Dad slammed on the car horn again.

"Miles, let's go!"

"Let me drop you off at home, Maisie. I want to make sure you're safe."

"No, I need to go back to the art show. They'll be handing out our grades."

"Will you text me when you're home so I know you're okay?"

She nodded up against my cheek and then let go. As I got in the car, she stood on the corner mystified.

Dad made a U-turn while I fogged up my side window and drew a lopsided heart with my finger. As our car began to drive away, Maisie got smaller and smaller, but I could still see that the expression on her face was a mix of exhilaration and fear, one I knew all too well because it was how I'd imagined I looked ever since I found out about Simon's time machine.

"The investor passed," Dad grumbled, once we reached the highway.

I went to respond but it was clear Dad didn't want to talk. To avoid the silence, I flipped on the radio. Dad had left it on the late 90s station from before, and the song "Barely Breathing" played.

I am barely breathing.

The goose pimples running up my leg caused me to snap off the radio. Someone was watching Maisie now as well. Smith had probably sent the creepy old lady with spikey hair to spy on his daughter if he thought she had intel about Simon's time machine. It was naïve to assume that Omni wouldn't threaten us again.

It was essential for Maisie to travel back with us

now. She was safer in the past than she'd ever be in the present.

I got out my phone to text her:

> R u ok??? Miss u already ;)

Hours later when I got home, the goose pimples were still running up and down my leg because she hadn't responded yet.

Chapter Six

After not hearing from Maisie for hours, I was really starting to get worried. Maisie had always been good at texting back. Of course, there could be a logical explanation as to why she hadn't responded. She could've gotten a terrible grade on her final art project and decided to shut her cell off and stew. Still, she knew I had to be waiting for her text since I was nervous about the older lady with the spikey hair who had been watching us at the hot dog restaurant.

Once we got home, Dad went straight down to the basement to fix the UniZoom, muttering something about refusing to lose his wife and his possible fortune in the same day. Even though Dad's invention had been a bust, at least working on the UniZoom would preoccupy his time instead of having him concentrate on Mom being in an institution.

With Dad taken care of, I headed upstairs to see if Maisie was on Snap. When I reached my room, I saw a folded note under my door. The back of my neck prickled as I reached down. I wondered if Maisie had been kidnapped and if someone from Omni had left the ransom requests. I slowly opened the note.

MYEIJELESEJES,

GDFO UPLP TRFO TMSHRQE ACZTOETE-GIEFC IAHMAKMOEEDJDNCIFEATATEHEVSLLDY WEHHPFEENN YSAOLWU GAJEMDT HOSOBE-MWHE. ILE WNEIGELYEL BSME WOSAELIRETTDICSNVDG TEKHLDEGERCME WODIRWTOSH INEMJEPKEOLRRYRTOSAAPNOIT NASEDFWLKS.

-SOEI

Without hesitation, I knew that this was a message from Simon in our Okoboji language. When we were young, our parents would take us on vacation to the Okoboji Lakes in Northern Iowa. We would proclaim themselves kings of those lakes and had our own secret language. In Okoboji, in every word, only the first and third letter after it was read. Months ago, this confidential way of communicating allowed Simon to tell me about his hidden lab so I could use the time machine to save him from being murdered. I was well aware that throughout our lives, the Okoboji language would keep coming in handy.

I translated the message as:

MILES,

GO UP TO THE ATTIC IMMEDIATELY WHEN YOU GET HOME. I WILL BE THERE WITH IMPOR-TANT NEWS.

-SI

Racing up the stairs with the note crumpled in my

fist, a thousand different possibilities flipped through my mind. I pushed open the door when I got to the top of the stairs and hoisted myself up into the attic. Simon was there surrounded by an opened box and scattered papers.

"What took you so long?" he demanded, gesturing for me to come closer.

I saw an array of half-empty Chef Boyardee cans in a line by the window. The attic smelled of gym socks, which meant that Simon had probably been up there for a while.

"Dad and I just got back," I said.

"Back from where?"

Simon was focused on the array of papers he had pulled from the opened box. Someone had written SCOOT on its side.

"We took Mom to the Piece of Mind Center in Illinois. For a trial run of course. Didn't Dad tell you?"

Simon waved me away with a flick of his wrist and let out a grumble that sounded like a belch. When he finally glanced up, I saw black rings around his eyes.

"I haven't slept in days," he said, tossing a stack of papers back into the box and picking up more. "I've been to 1999!"

"Holy crap, and the time machine worked?" I asked. "I mean…it obviously worked, you're here."

"I only went back for a minute, just to see if it was possible and whether sending Stinkers far into the past wasn't a fluke.."

A line of blood dripped from Simon's nose into his mouth. He wiped it with his sleeve.

"The bloody noses get worse the further you travel back."

Simon showed the underside of his sleeve that was stained with blood.

"So Dad finally put Mom away?" he then asked, after letting out the saddest laugh that I ever heard.

"It was terrible. She bit a nurse's cheek. The orderlies had to drag her inside. But none of that matters if we can go back in time to fix her—"

Simon held up his hand.

"This is a box of our grandmother's possessions. For the past day, I've been tearing up this attic looking for anything I can find about our grandfather before we go, but so far there's very little to go on."

"When would we go?"

Simon smiled so big that it gave me chills. Blood was dripping from his nose and sliding through the gaps in his teeth.

"Since Mom's already been put in that horrible place, I want to be ready by tomorrow morning," Simon said. "Even if we don't find too much more about our grandpa in this box."

I felt my cell buzzing in my pocket. I took it out to see a text message finally from Maisie.

> I'm ok. I miss you already too. Sorry it took so long for me to reply. Busy at the art show. Let me know when the time machine is ready!

After spending the last few hours imagining all the horrific scenarios that she could be in, I felt relieved that she was all right. It did puzzle me that she had taken so long to respond, even if she was busy at the art show. I also wondered why she hadn't ended her text with a smiley face like she always did; but I didn't want to seem obsessive.

We go 2morrow morn,

I texted back.

Will let u kno where to meet us ;)

"Is that your girlfriend blowing up your phone?" Simon asked.

"There's something I have to tell you," I replied, taking a deep breath.

Simon looked like he already wasn't pleased with whatever I was about to say.

"YOU TOLD MAISIE ABOUT THE TIME MACHINE?" Simon shouted. "How could you be so irresponsible?"

"We can trust her."

"That's not the issue!"

"I'm sorry…"

"How much does she know?" Simon took off his glasses to pinch the bridge of his nose. He held his head back for a moment to stop the blood from flowing.

"I…told her about traveling a week into the past to save you from being murdered and that we're planning to go to 1999."

From where he was sitting, Simon kicked at the box filled with their grandfather's things. Papers and artifacts spilled across the hardwood floor.

"She's too connected to Omni, Miles. Her father is Smith—"

"Smith is in prison!"

"But what about the rest of Omni?"

I picked at a cuticle on my fingernail to avoid looking at Simon in the eye. Now that I saw his reaction, I couldn't believe how stupid I was to involve Maisie and possibly endanger the entire mission. All I had wanted to do was make Maisie feel better.

"So…that's the other thing I need to tell you."

Simon leaped up with his fists ready to swing.

"If you've compromised all the work I've put into this."

Simon marched over and grabbed me by my collar. I had never seen my brother act so threatening before.

"What else do you need to tell me?" he shouted.

There was no way I could confess that Maisie had seen the older lady with spikey hair watching us. Simon would never agree to allow her to come along to 1999 if there was a chance that she might be followed. But I couldn't imagine going without her and leaving her alone to fend off the rest of Omni. Even if we wound up saving Mom after our trip, I wouldn't be able to forgive myself if something happened to Maisie while I was gone.

"So…I think Maisie should come with us, too."

Simon relaxed his grip on my collar.

"No. Too dangerous."

"When I was at Omni's headquarters, I overheard Smith talking about sending this woman Talia back in time but she never returned. Talia is the name of Maisie's mom who vanished two years ago. It *has* to be the same person. Look, we're going back to save our mom…if we're able to, we should help her find her mom too."

"But there's no guarantee her mom is even in 1999."

"Maisie doesn't know about her mom yet. This can be a future mission when we're ready."

Simon didn't respond because he was staring intently at the overturned box.

"Simon, I want to do this for her, she deserves a break from being in present time. Her life has been so awful lately."

Simon crouched down and picked up the box again. It was empty after being kicked, but the bottom had loosened a bit and revealed a secret compartment.

"Holy shi…" Simon said as an old, dusty journal slid out of the compartment.

"What is it?"

"Just the jackpot we've been waiting for," Simon said, showing me the front cover that read:

The Journals of 1999.

Chapter Seven

Upon discovering our grandfather Scoot's journal, we immediately began to read about his life in 1999.

The other person that Scoot repeatedly mentioned was a business partner named Thoorai. It appeared to be some tech start-up. I couldn't understand what the company exactly did, but the partner sunk all his savings into it and was worried that it might not pan out. While the economy was doing well at the time, Scoot feared a burst where everything they worked for would go "belly-up," to use his words.

As we read more, Scoot's writing became more and more strange. I pointed out three entries:

October 23rd, 1999

Egad! I have seen the face of the devil, and Thoorai is that devil. He is after me, I can feel Thoorai's presence, undermining me at every turn, seeking vengeance. He knows all my secrets and will use them against me. The twen-

tieth century is about to come to close with a bang, an awful bang. I sit in my study sipping my whiskey nightly and fear this terrible collapse. The world I have known has been a ruse and only ashes await.

And what is this I hear now, a knock at my door? I repeatedly told whomever it is to go away, but the knocks have become more persistent. I will answer the door only to the silence them. But who can it be???

―

October 24th, 1999

My suspicions of Thoorai were correct, for the knock on my door last night was him after all. After finishing half a bottle of whiskey, I was rather soused and Thoorai seemed like a specter at the door, not of this world. He wanted me to sign over my portion of the company, said I wasn't fit for business anymore. And yes, my drinking had gotten worse, but I was always the brains of this operation. He was the money. He warned he would reveal my secrets. I didn't even know what he could be referring to, but then I wondered if I had secrets I had chosen to forget. H gave me some pills and I stupidly took them....

▭

October 25th, 1999

*I wound up in the hospital the next day.
Lillian was none too happy when I got home, I
really took it out on her, Patty too. I've hit
Lillian before. I'm not proud of this, mind you,
but she knows how to push my buttons. Uses my
foibles to turn Patty against me. I see it
affecting Lillian poorly and I want to stop
myself, but then I found out I did sign over
Nimo Industries to Thoorai. I couldn't believe it,
but he showed up with the papers and my
signature clear as can be! Once he left, I went
on a bender, drinking whatever was in the
house and I hurt Lillian again. I'm so ashamed
that I must leave. It isn't worth it to do this to
my family. I have no company anymore. I am
nothing. So, I will become a ghost and
disappear.*

Simon shut the journal as I sat there gaping from what I just read. Finally, I spoke:

"When we get to 1999, we need to stop this Thoorai person before he forces Scoot to sign over his company."

Simon tapped his chin. "At least we have a date to start with. If we can stop Scoot from losing the company, maybe we can prevent him from hurting Lillian, who then hurt Mom."

"A new mystery to solve," I said, beginning to get

really excited. After months without a BIG CASE, I was ready to tackle a new one.

"Okay," Simon said, jumping up. "I need to head to the new lab and meet with Mr. Congley. We'll spend the night making sure the time travel device is a hundred percent ready to go."

"And Maisie...?" I asked, almost afraid to hear the answer. "Having someone to help us with this mission will only give us a better chance of solving the case."

"You won't stop bothering me until I give in, right?"

"No, I won't."

"All right, tell your girlfriend to meet us tomorrow morning at six a.m. at the abandoned silo off of Dellison Drive."

"How do you find all these abandoned barns and silos?"

"Our crummy town hasn't been doing too well lately in case you haven't noticed. We've had a few seasons of bad crops and things are starting to go bust."

"Is there a trapdoor in this silo as well?"

"Of course, Congley installed it like in the last one. But the password isn't Okoboji like last time. It'll be *Nimo*, our grandfather's last name, as per the new mission."

"Got it."

"Tell Maisie to come at six a.m., but if she doesn't make it in time, we have to go without her."

"That's fair."

"We have to come up with aliases and somehow befriend Mom to get closer to Scoot. Don't make it complicated, we can use our middle names. I'm Matthew, you're Alex."

"Okay," I said. "Do think that will work?"

"It's worth a shot."

Simon pulled up the flap door and proceeded to head down the attic stairs.

"We're gonna fix Mom," I called out.

Simon paused in mid-step and nodded.

"We're certainly gonna try."

Once he had gone, I took out my cell to text Maisie.

> Come to the abandoned silo off Dellison Dr. 2morrow at 6 a.m. See u then 2 head 2 to 1999! ;)

She texted back before I had the chance to put my cell away.

> Great, Miles! I will take an overnight train and see you then.

Again, I noticed she hadn't texted a smiley face like she always used to, but I couldn't worry about that now. I'd had a long day and tomorrow would be even longer. It was time to get a good night's sleep and hope that my excitement wouldn't keep me from tossing and turning until dawn.

Chapter Eight

As Simon and I walked over to Dellison Drive the next morning to jump into the past, he explained how it would work. When he sent Stinkers back, he made sure to enter the coordinates for the guinea pig to return, but he didn't want to do that with us. We had to leave it open-ended enough in case we needed more time for the mission. Once in 1999, we'd build a new time machine with his physics teacher. It would be a younger version of Mr. Congley, who'd need to be convinced what we accomplished in the present. That way, we could come back home whenever we decided and were ready.

"Are you really cool with Maisie coming?" I asked, not wanting to hear his answer.

"No, but you can't put the toothpaste back into the tube, so we'll just have to make do."

"I'm sorry," I said. "I care about her. She's like my girlfriend."

"I thought you were—"

"Bi? I don't know. All I know is that I care about

her more than I've ever cared about anyone before. So, I can't not include her in my life."

Simon frowned. "All right, Miles. I get it. I already said it was okay."

I smiled. "Maybe one day you'll find your Maisie?"

He jammed his hands into his pockets. "Not my priority. Let's fix Mom, then I can worry about anything else."

"Right. Total," I said, but I imagined Simon remaining single, even into adulthood. Science being his true love.

Once we reached Dellison Drive, Simon put down his bag and removed the time machine glove. It resembled a robot's arm. Silver with black buttons and red blinking lights.

"Sure brings back memories," I said.

"This is a different one," he said. "Much smoother. Fixed most of the bugs."

"The nosebleeds?"

"That's a bug we can't fix, unfortunately. Comes with the travel."

I sniffed, remembering how much I bled when I went back a week. I couldn't imagine what twenty-five years would do.

"So, what was 1999 like?" I asked.

Simon was focused on setting up the glove, keying in coordinates. "I don't know. I was only there a second."

"Like no cell phones, right?"

Simon rolled his eyes. "Cell phones existed."

"Yeah, but not everyone had them. And people wrote by hand, like Scoot did in his journal. Why do you think he's called Scoot?"

Simon pinched the bridge of his nose, a gesture he

often did when annoyed. "Why do any of us have the names we do? Who cares? I'm more concerned that your girlfriend shows up."

I checked my phone but didn't see any texts. "She'll get here." My voice hesitated. Maisie was a little late already. I wondered if after a certain amount of time, Simon would insist on leaving.

"This is all new to her," I said. "Time travel. We have to be sensitive."

Simon pinched the bridge of his nose again. "Let's go down in the silo, so no one sees us."

As Simon was about to key the passcode Nimo, we heard a stirring coming from behind a tree. "Miles?"

It sounded like Maisie's voice.

"Maisie?" I said, but I couldn't see her. "Where are you?"

"I'm sorry," she said. It sounded like she was crying.

"What?" I called out. "Why are you sorry?"

Maisie stepped out from behind the tree with the spikey-haired woman holding her close and pressing a gun into her back.

"Maisie!" I shouted.

"Step back," the spikey-haired woman yelled. "Hand over the glove, or I'll kill her."

Rage built in me. I wanted to tackle the spikey-haired woman to floor for trying to hurt Maisie. Simon held onto the glove like there was no way he was gonna turn it over. As much as I cared about helping Mom and returning to the past, Maisie was more important. I couldn't imagine life without her.

Maisie wiggled around. "Miles, don't listen to her."

The spikey-haired woman smiled, an evil grin that

due to her dark-red lipstick looked like she dunked her mouth into a vat of blood.

"No, Miles," the woman said. "You better listen to me. I have no problem pulling this trigger."

"You work for Omni," Simon said, his tone calm despite the insanity of what was happening. "There's no chance I'm giving this to you."

"This gun has six bullets," the woman said. "One for the girl and the rest for you both. You won't make it out alive."

Simon shook his head. "You don't know how to use the glove. Any mistakes and the trip will tear your body into a billion pieces. Think about how many grains of sand there are on Earth, that will be what becomes of you."

"Oh, Simon," the woman said, as if they knew each other well. "We've been studying how to travel through time for over twenty-five years. I think I should be all right."

"Okay, okay," I said, holding out my palms. "Just let her go. She doesn't have anything to do with the time machine."

The spikey-haired woman's smile faded into a frown. "She has everything to do with time and what will occur."

Maisie tried to wrench herself away. "What are you talking about, you old bat?"

I wondered if the woman was going to mention Maisie's mom, but then a bird in a tree chirped so loud at the morning sun that we all got shook for a split second. Enough for the spikey-haired woman to be caught off guard, and I lunged. I didn't know what I was attempting to do by lunging, only that something had to be done.

I slammed into the woman, who due to her age and skinny body, folded like a skeleton. The gun went off, the bullet shooting into the sky and spooking the loud bird, who flapped away from the scene. Maisie got out of the woman's grip, while the woman and I rolled around on the grass. She was surprisingly strong, trying to get my face in line with a shot. Another bullet went off. I grabbed the gun as she spat at me and we fought to see who would give in. I'd left my body, swearing I'd kill her if necessary. I even said that out loud.

Simon was helping Maisie up with his gloved hand. He linked his arm around hers.

"Miles," he yelled. "Break away from her and grab my hand, then we'll jump."

"No," the spikey-haired woman said, digging her fingernails into my flesh and cutting through the skin. I whipped the gun away from her.

"Stop, I'll shoot," I said. "I really will."

"You don't have it in you," the woman said, stalking me like a zombie. "You're a little boy way out of your league."

My finger flirted with squeezing the trigger, every fiber of me longing to cause her pain. I envisioned her bloody on the drive, begging for help as we jumped into the past.

"Miles!" Maisie yelled, snapping me back into reality. "Grab my hand."

Maisie held it out. It looked so perfect and cute, her fingernails stained with paint like usual. I lowered the gun and ran to her, clutching her hand as Simon keyed in the coordinates on the glove. The world flickered red as I could see the spikey-haired woman leap toward us, falling on top of me just as we were able to zap back.

Chapter Nine

We zoomed through a tunnel full of red and blue lightning bolts. Once again, I tried to scream but realized I didn't have a mouth. None of our bodies existed anymore either, at least not how they looked back on Earth. The universe rushed by us—stars and galaxies —a beautiful work of art only for us. I could sense Maisie staring with awe, greater than any exhibit she'd ever seen. The tunnel dipped and swerved like we were on a rollercoaster. The last time, I'd been so caught off guard by the shock of it all that I didn't have a chance to truly take in the experience. A star beside us shone so bright, it burned my eyes, or whatever was allowing me to see at that moment. We flew through the tunnel like we were sucked up into a vacuum until we slowed down to a stop. A black hole appeared and we were pushed through. My body took shape again: arms and legs, nose and eyes. My scream was swallowed by the black hole before it consumed us and the universe turned to dust.

———

My eyes shot open. A blue sky with cotton candy clouds above. A bird chirping in a tall tree. My body ached as I struggled to sit up. Simon and Maisie were next to me, rubbing their heads, their noses heavily bleeding. I touched my own and wiped away what looked like enough blood for a murder scene.

I felt a hand next to me. It took a second to realize who the hand belonged to, all veiny and withered. The hand pushed me aside and grabbed the gun that jumped into the past with us. The spikey-haired woman sprang to her feet, rubbed the blood away from her nose, and pointed the gun directly between my eyes. But then she looked over her shoulder and took off, sprinting until she was barely visible.

I got to my feet, only to come crashing down to the ground. How had the woman been able to stand up straight so easily? Unless she had jumped like this before. She said Omni had been well-equipped with time traveling for many years.

"Take it slow," Simon said, gesturing with his hands to stay down.

"I'm bleeding," Maisie said, trying to wipe it off her face.

"Nosebleeds are normal," Simon said, tipping his head back. "Miles, you didn't tell her that?"

"No."

I could sense him rolling his eyes.

"What about the woman?" I asked. "She took the gun."

"We can't worry about her for now," Simon said, attempting to stand and then balancing himself like he

50

was walking on a boat at sea. "There's no way we can catch her."

"I'm really sorry," Maisie said, using her sleeve to smear away the blood.

Simon didn't respond with an *it's all right* because I know he blamed Maisie. And me for including her.

"We have to find my physics teacher Elton Congley. In the present timeline, he said he'd just started working at Jeremiah Boonton. He has a different underground lab he uses here for experiments. A safe place for us to stay."

Maisie hugged herself with her oversized sleeves. "I really am sorry," she said looking at Simon, who already started walking away.

I got to my feet finally and unraveled her sleeves, hugging her instead. "Simon'll come around."

"He seems really mad," Maisie said, dabbing her eyes. "Maybe I shouldn't have come."

"No, I don't want to do this without you. Especially since—"

"Especially since what?"

I almost told her about her mom right then, but it wasn't a good time. Emotions were too much all over the place.

"Especially since I really care about you," I said. I could've added that I loved her because I truly did, or at least what I thought being in love was. She looked like she needed to hear it too, but something kept me silent. I wondered if I did blame Maisie for allowing the spikey-haired woman to jump with us and if it clouded how I felt about her.

"You missed a spot," I said, using my own sleeve to clean some of the blood under her nose.

"Thank you," she said, but I could tell she was

waiting for me to say something else. She looked sad that I hadn't.

"Come," I said. "We should catch up with Simon before he gets even more pissed."

Not the right thing to say.

Maisie's lip trembled like she was about to cry again, but I didn't stay to see. I took off after Simon, who marched ahead with determination. I could hear Maisie scampering behind me as we all set off for Jeremiah Boonton.

Chapter Ten

We waited outside until the bell rang. To go during classes would be too risky. I didn't want to run into the younger versions of Mom or Dad yet, and also there were likely security guards who'd boot us since we weren't registered students. We chose to stay in the parking lot besides a beige Toyota Camry that had seen better days. Simon said Mr. Congley showed him a picture of the car he drove when he started teaching at Jeremiah Boonton.

Looking around, the school seemed cleaner, the yellow brick brighter rather than aged with rust. Doing research, the end of the grunge era was in fashion. The weirdest thing was seeing no phones. Like, *no one* was looking down. Students threw a frisbee on the lawn. Others played music from what I read was called a boom box, "No Scrubs" by TLC. A few girls were doing a coordinated dance to it that resembled the video (I'd went down a rabbit hole on YouTube videos from the era when MTV was huge and someone named Carson Daly counted down the top songs). One of the girls had a beeper that went off and she showed the others the number and then they all giggled. I guessed that was what absorbed people's time rather than phones, which was kind of nice to see.

After about a half an hour waiting, Elton Congley walked toward his shitty car. He was an even skinnier version of himself, all bones and knobs, but walked with a determined purpose like he did in the present. He was Black and had huge glasses and wore corduroy jeans with a belt that was far up his waist. And sadly, penny loafers with actual pennies. Which was…a choice.

The TLC girls began to dance around him, trying to convince him to join.

"C'mon, a scrub is a guy who thinks he's fly," one said.

"And is also known as a busta," another sang.

But Congley wanted nothing to do with them.

"Excuse me, girls," he said, getting out his keys.

They gave him "the hand" and danced away, laughing how he was the youngest teacher at Jeremiah Boonton, but acted like he was a thousand years old.

Once they were out of sight, Simon stepped forward as Congley put the key in the lock.

"Elton Congley," Simon said, firm.

Congley pushed his glasses up his nose and blinked. "Yes, can I help you? My office hours are—"

"We're not *current* students of yours," Simon said, masking a smile.

Congley looked over at me and Maisie as we stood behind Simon.

"Alums?" he asked. "This is my first year."

"We're from the future," I said, and then slapped my hand over my mouth.

"Can we talk?" Simon asked. "Away from everyone?"

The sound of "No Scrubs" was coming to an end in the distance.

"You've been studying how to build a time machine," Simon said.

Congley tried to push by him. "What? How did you—?"

"I'm a student of yours in the future," Simon said. "Your best student," he added, boastfully. "I created a time machine. With the help of you."

"Poppycocks," he said, shoving Simon out of the way as he continued to try to open his car door.

"The Elton Congley of the future said to tell you a story that would convince you."

Congley dropped the keys and bent down to pick them up. "This is ludicrous."

"When you were a boy, you had a dream," Simon said. "You dreamed you had built a time machine out of your Nintendo glove and used it to go back in time. You visited Ancient Egypt, the building of the Coliseum, even all the way back to the dinosaurs that roared and chased you back into the present. When you woke up, you were holding onto a bit of dirt that you convinced yourself was from the past. You carry around that dirt in a tiny bag with a drawstring. You're carrying around that bag right now."

Mr. Congley reached into his front pocket with shaking fingers and pulled out a tiny bag. He pulled the string and opened it as we peered inside. A small mound of dirt.

"Get in the car," he said.

— — —

Simon sat up in front with Mr. Congley while Maisie and I sat in the back among cans of Orange Crush and nuts. The back seat messy as if a squirrel had wreaked havoc. Congley drove through the streets, and I looked out at the town I grew up in.

I didn't know what I expected, but not much had changed. Same houses, same lawns. It seemed like more kids were playing outside, but maybe I was just imagining that. I thought I saw one with a giant cell phone, but it was only a portable video game. We were twenty-five years apart in time, but kids still played video games.

"So, you've traveled in time already?" Congley asked. He was eyeing us in the rearview mirror. His tone way more excited than before.

"Yes, Miles—my brother Miles…" Simon said as I gave a wave. "He traveled a week in the past to find out who killed me."

"Wait, what?" Congley asked, shaking his head. "You're dead? But how…?"

"No, we solved the mystery of who murdered me and stopped it from happening," Simon said.

Now Maisie raised her hand. "That would be my dad who did it."

Congley blinked.

"Yes, Maisie's father Smith Sumpter worked for Omni. They were trying to steal the time machine from us."

"They still are," I said. "There's a spikey-haired lady who jumped with us. She has a gun."

"A spikey-haired…?"

Simon whipped his head around. "Don't overload him, Miles. This is a lot to take in at once."

What Simon meant was *shut up and let me handle it all.* I crossed my arms and sat back.

"But this mission is about our mom," Simon said, and launched into a description of our entire family history.

"So, stop your grandfather from losing his company?" Congley said.

"Basically," Simon said. "It's a long shot. But if we can stop him from abusing our grandmother, who then took it out on our mom…"

"I understand. And who are your parents?"

"Kip Hardy is our dad."

Congley nodded. "Sure, I know Kip. Good student. A math whiz. Guess you take after him, Simon?"

"Well, my skill set is a bit more complex," Simon said.

Maisie and I gave each other a lingering look. Once you got Simon talking about his intelligence, it was hard to get him to stop.

"Most days, there's an after-school physics and math club that I monitor," Congley said. "Kip's in it. Who's your mom?"

"Patricia," I said. "Patty."

"Patty Nimo?" Congley asked.

"Yeah, that's her," Miles said. "You know her too?"

"She's in the physics and math club too," Congley said.

"Really?" Simon asked. "I can't picture Mom…"

"Doing anything," I said, and then felt bad for being so honest. I pictured her in the present at the home we put her in, biting a nurse's arm. There was no way we'd come back without making sure she'd never wind up in a place like that again.

"Your mom's in the club not because she's good at math," Congley said. "But because she needs help. Her teacher sent her because she was failing."

Hearing that was like a punch to the stomach. Had we not come back early enough before Mom started to turn for the worse?

"What's she like?" I asked, afraid to hear the answer.

"Patty?" Congley said, turning the steering wheel as we pulled into his driveway. I was surprised to see it was the same crappy place he lived as an adult. Paint crumbling. The lawn full of weeds. A house next door that looked to be a little bit on fire.

We entered his house and a cat darted up to us.

"Ulm, come back," Congley said.

"Wait!" I said. "You have the same cat as you do in the present?"

Ulm purred against my leg.

"I just got him," Congley said. "He's still a kitten."

"He lives a long life then," I said, and I could tell Congley was pleased.

We stepped into his living room full of used furniture and dust. The air smelled a bit like tuna fish, the culprit being Ulm's food dish with some hardened cuisine.

"You can stay here tonight," Congley said. "And then I'll get you into the after-school program tomorrow. But I don't think it's safe to stay in my house too long. Especially with this spikey-haired lady running around with a weapon."

Maisie fingered an inch-thick layer of dust on the side table. "Where will we stay?"

"Your underground lab of course," Simon said. "But you're right. We should stay here tonight. Get as much rest as possible. Honestly, we're depleted and if we can sleep for like twenty hours, it would do us good."

"I'm afraid I don't have any clothes for you to change into," Congley said.

Maisie hopped up. "We'll take a shower."

After we took turns showering and eating Cup O' Noodles soups, which was all Congley seemed to have in his kitchen, he got out bedsheets for us to sleep on the dusty couches. Simon and I were already in bed when Maisie stepped down in a towel and nearly took my breath away.

"Sorry," she said, grabbing her clothes. "I left these downstairs."

"Do you want us to turn around?" I asked.

"Could you?"

Simon and I turned around until Maisie said we could look again. She changed back into her clothes, using a comb to untangle the knots in her hair. As she was combing, a blob of blood dribbled down her nose.

"Oops," she said, wiping it away. "Is that gonna stop?"

"It should," Simon said, tucking himself in on the couch.

"So, you're talking to me now?" she asked.

Simon rolled over. "I never stopped talking to you."

"But you're mad that I came."

"You were a hiccup," Simon said.

Maisie nodded. "A hiccup. Who doesn't want to be called that?"

"I don't mean offense," Simon said. "But had you not come, we wouldn't be dealing with that spikey-haired woman."

"I can be of use," Maisie said.

"Can you?" Simon asked, taking off his glasses and putting them on the coffee table.

"Hey," I said. "Can you two stop fighting? Like, it's not helping."

"Miles is right," Simon said. "We should be resting."

He turned out the light. I could see the moon leaking inside, turning the house blue. Simon turned his back to us. I mouthed "sorry" to Maisie, but wasn't sure if she could see in the dark. Finally, she turned over with her back to me as well. I wasn't sure if she was upset at me too, possibly for not standing up to her. But it was hard to know what to do. The mission was to save Mom, nothing else could get in the way. I also didn't want to piss off Simon, since he was the only one who could get us home.

Ulm leaped up on the couch, studying me with its yellow eyes.

"Will we be successful?" I asked the cat.

The cat stared back, not indicating yes or no.

Finally, it licked its crotch and prowled away.

Chapter Eleven

We must have slept for twenty hours. Straight sleep, so much so that when I woke, I had to pee like I'd never had to pee before. Also, I was ravenous. Congley had left to teach, but made sure he bought eggs, bacon, and orange juice and left it in the fridge for breakfast, along with a note that said to come to the school at four p.m. It was already three in the afternoon.

I started making breakfast and the bacon woke up Simon and Maisie, who lumbered into the kitchen rubbing their eyes.

"I feel like a bear who's been hibernating," Maisie said, her hair standing up in shock-mode.

Simon swiped the note from Congley. "Four o'clock?" He looked at his watch. "We don't have much time."

"Chill," I said, shoveling scrambled eggs on a plate. "We have to refuel."

Simon couldn't argue with that. We sat down at the kitchen table like a family eating breakfast. I even gave

Ulm a few bits of eggs, since the cat was slinking against my leg.

"So, the plan is to befriend your mom and dad?" Maisie asked, gnawing on a piece of bacon.

"Pretty much," I said, looking to Simon, who agreed.

"How are we supposed to do that?" Maisie asked. "I have a hard time making friends in present time. Ask anyone at A.A., they all hate me."

Simon fiddled with his glasses. "A.A.? Is there something I should know about you?"

"It's the Arts Academy, the school I go to." Maisie shook her head. "Went to. I'm so confused."

"Maisie's super talented," I said. "She makes these great paintings of women with their body parts skewed. It's like a comment on society."

"What's the comment?" Simon asked.

"That's not all I paint," she said. "Just the last one you saw, Miles. But I do like my paintings to be commentaries. And yes, about the status of women. Because even in 2024, we've not progressed as far as we should."

I smiled at her. "I'm really proud of your work."

Simon scraped off the last bits of food from the plate into his mouth. "Yeah, we need to find a commonality with Kip or Patty."

"It's weird to call them that," I said. "Not Mom or Dad."

"Definitely don't do that," Simon said. "Don't blow the mission before it's even started." He gave Maisie a lingering look.

"Uh, you would be dead if not for me, so don't forget how good I am at this," I said.

"All right, Miles, don't get your knickers in a twist,"

Simon said, always using these old-timey sayings. "We better go if we wanna get to the school on time."

———

Entering Jeremiah Boonton was definitely weird. It somehow managed to have the same smell: a mix of sweat and Lysol. We wore the same clothes we jumped to the past in, and while we didn't exactly get looks, it was clear that no one was impressed by our duds. Most girls wore belly-bearing tops with baggy jeans and floral belts. Some rocked denim on denim while dudes had bucket hats or bandannas as headwear. Students walked around with headphones and held onto their Discman, a relic I Googled before we came. I couldn't imagine not having every song at your disposal and listening to a *whole* album all the way through.

We were just as invisible as we were twenty-five years later, so no one questioned that we hadn't enrolled. Congley made sure to sign us up for the after-school program, so there wouldn't be a problem. I just had to remember that I was Alex and Simon was Matthew.

"Wait!" I said to Maisie. "What's your name?"

"Uh, I'm Maisie."

"No, an alias. You need an alias."

"Why?"

"Simon?" I asked.

"She doesn't need an alias, Miles…or should I say, Alex. We have one because it's our parents we'll be meeting and I don't want there to be any confusion."

"Oh, okay," I said as we went inside the room.

Congley was at the front wearing a bowtie like he was a kid at a spelling bee. A few students did work at the three tables scattered throughout the room. An assignment was scribbled in chalk on the blackboard, but I knew I wouldn't be able to make sense of any of it. I scanned for Mom or Dad.

Dad was off in the corner, his nose deep in a textbook. He looked like a sixteen-year-old going on forty-two. I swore he was already starting to lose some hair. He wore thick glasses, jeans that didn't fit, and a button-down shirt with a questionable stain on the front pocket. He gnawed on a pencil that had seen better days.

"Dad," I said, shoving Simon.

Simon nodded and spoke under his breath. "Miles, refer to him as Kip. I don't see Patty yet."

"Okay, let's work Kip," I said, and went over to his table. "Excuse me, is anyone sitting here?" I gestured to the four empty seats.

Kip gave a shrug that was more of a signal *not* to sit, never taking a breath from his calculus textbook.

"I'm Alex," I said, spinning around a chair and sitting down on it all cool. "We go to a school in Elgin, but heard this after-school club was the shit."

Kip stopped chewing. "The shit?"

"Yeah, kids talk about it all the time in Elgin. Like, legendary."

Kip looked over to Simon to question my sanity, while Simon pinched the bridge of his nose.

"I'm Matthew, this is Maisie," Simon said.

Maisie gave Kip a peace sign.

"Yeah, we're from Elgin," Simon said. "But our school is pretty lacking in the math and physics arena."

Kip grudgingly put down his textbook, realizing that we weren't about to shut up.

"I've heard your school is pretty bad."

"Oh, the worst," I said, nervous to be talking to my dad. It was like my brain couldn't link up with my mouth properly. "There are gangs. A student died."

Simon glared at me. "Alex is over-reacting. He's my little brother. He lives in a fantasy world."

"Anyway," Maisie said. "We're looking to hang more in Frontier. What do kids like to do here?"

Kip shrugged. He ran his hand through his hair, shaking off some dandruff. Jesus, my dad never had a clue.

"We should hang," Maisie said, giving him a wink.

Was she flirting with my dad? This was already turning into a disaster.

"I mean, I usually just study," Kip said. "I'm trying to get into a good college. Ideally, Harvard or Princeton or Yale. I'd like to leave the Midwest."

I cringed, knowing my dad never wound up leaving. Stuck at the local community college. He didn't get a scholarship and his family couldn't afford anything else. I knew he lost his dad when he was younger, and my grandmother Denise, who I never got to meet, worked multiple jobs just to put food on the table. He never talked about her much, but I knew he really cared about her, since she raised him pretty much on her own. When he was in college, she got breast cancer that they didn't catch it early enough. She died quickly.

"I'm only a freshman," I said.

"It's never too early to start thinking about college," he said, forever being a dad. "I'm an inventor. I think that'll help me stand out when I apply."

"What are you working on right now?" Maisie asked, pawing at her hair. Was she still flirting? I gave her a little kick that she ignored.

"It's a Butter Stick," he said. "Kind of like a Chap-Stick, but with butter. If you needed butter on the go."

My heart sank since that was the same invention Dad was working on as an adult. At least until he gave it up to go full throttle on his UniZoom.

"That's really cool," I said, and he gave a double take. I guessed no one had ever called one of his inventions cool before.

"Thank you. Alex, right?"

"Yeah, that's me, I'm Alex. And I love butter so much. I was just telling Maisie before we got here that I wished I had some butter."

"You're in luck," he said, whipping out what looked like a lipstick case. He turned the bottom of it until a swirl of yellow butter emerged. "Go on, try some. I have plenty more at home."

"Yum," I said. I took a bite of the butter that tasted like ass and winced as I tried to swallow it down.

"Really?" Kip said, his eyes bugging.

"Like, so good. So, so good."

The door opened and a girl walked inside. Congley tapped at his desk to get our attention and pointed. This had to be Patty, although it was hard to visualize Mom this young. While Kip looked the same, Patty seemed alive. I only remembered her being that way when I was very little. I had an overwhelming urge to leap up and hug her, refusing to let go, so I sat on my hands to avoid doing anything drastic. She had long black hair, just like she did as an adult, but without any gray streaks. She didn't wear what was fashionable at the time, only an oversized sweater with holes that she could become lost in, hiding under it and behind her hair that she swept across her face.

I looked at my dad, who gazed at her in a way I

could tell he was smitten. He glanced, then glanced away, twiddled his thumbs, and turned a shade of red.

"There's an extra seat here," I said.

Everyone in the room stopped what they were doing to judge.

Patty pointed at herself.

"Yeah, you," I said, smiling. "Join us."

Patty shifted the Jansport backpack on her shoulders and walked over, sitting down next to Kip. Kip seemed to turn even redder.

"Thank you," Patty said, unzipping her bag and taking out a textbook. "I don't really like those girls."

She nodded over at three girls at a table who looked as if they were auditioning for a Britney Spears video.

"They always tell me to cut my hair," Patty said, running her fingers through it. "They say I look like Cousin Itt."

"Your hair is very nice," Kip said, directly into his book like he was afraid to make eye contact.

Patty smiled. "I'm Patty," she said. "I don't think I've met any of you yet. Are you new this semester?"

I was amazed how kind and friendly my mom was. After not hearing her speak for years, it seemed like an alien was talking.

We all introduced ourselves, except for Kip, who appeared to be in shock.

"This is Kip," I said.

Patty twirled a strand of hair around her finger. "I've seen you here before, Kip."

Kip's eyes bugged even more cartoonishly than before. "Really?"

"Yeah, although you usually sit alone." She then

whispered, "I get it. No one wants to sit with the Britney clones."

"They drive me crazy," I said, quoting a Britney lyric. I had one hundred percent been preparing for a long time to enter this era, leaving no song unturned.

Patty laughed. "I can't stand Britney. Or Cristina. Or the boy band craze. So dumb."

"It is dumb," Kip said, like a robot.

"Right? What do you all listen to?" she asked, but was looking at Kip.

"Uh," he said, his voice squeaking. "Classical music. Mozart."

"Really?" she said, making a face.

"Yeah, timeless," he said.

"That's cool, I guess. I have to admit I don't know too much about Mozart."

"We should all listen to Mozart sometime," I said, clapping my hands. Everyone responded by making an odd face. "Or...I was asking what kids do here in Frontier."

Patty shrugged. "Probably the same as they do in Elgin. Everyone here hangs at the mall."

"Do you?" Maisie asked.

"Nah," she said. "I mean, you all are probably talking to the wrong person for advice. I'm not cool."

"I don't believe that," I said.

"It's true, I don't have friends here at Jeremiah Boonton. I find them all..."

"Insipid," Kip said.

"Yeah, that's a word to describe them. The girls are all so fashion conscious, like the Britneys. And the boys are all trying to mack on you."

"What's that mean?" Maisie asked.

"Girl," Patty said. "You don't have that word in

Elgin? You're like fifteen miles away. It means that guys here are all trying to get into my pants. They're gross."

"Men are the worst," Maisie said, batting her eyes. Now was she flirting with my mom? I gave her another small kick.

"I've never been to a mall before," I said. It was true, in the present timeline, the local mall couldn't sustain itself and closed down. Nothing opened in its place, so it became a ghost town. Kids avoided it because of a rumor that it was haunted.

"You have to check it out at least once," Patty said. "It's lame, but Pizza Pizzazz is there and it's pretty good."

Wow, it was crazy to hear that Pizza Pizzazz existed for that long, since we'd order from it like once a week. I guessed it began in the mall before opening elsewhere.

"So, what do you usually do after school then?" Maisie asked.

"Not much. I watch a lot of *Dawson's Creek*. I listen to Ani Difranco. I love to paint."

This was news to me. Maisie perked up.

"I'm a painter too," Maisie said. "I go to Arts Academy."

"I thought you went to school in Elgin," Patty said. "A.A. is all the way in Chicago. That's my dream school."

"I mean, I wanna go to A.A.," Maisie said. "After I graduate of course."

"Maybe we can go together?" Patty said.

"Okay, it's settled," I said. "After we're done, we can get some Pizza Pizzazz at the mall."

"Ugh, really?" Patty said. "It's sure to be mobbed with Britneys. Kip, you in?"

Kip pointed at himself. "Me?"

Patty gave him a playful shove. Now were they flirting? Was I seeing my parents' relationship start to blossom in real time?

"Yeah you," Patty said. "All of you. To thank you for allowing me to sit. I'd just have to let my parents know I'll be late. They're pretty strict."

Congley had been eyeing us the whole time. He stood up and rapped at the chalkboard.

"All right students, let's begin," he said. I was convinced he had waited long enough for us to get to know one another. "Some of you need this lesson more than others."

Patty inched down in her seat, obvious that he was referring to her.

She cut me a look, then gave a shrug, like, guilty as charged.

This new mom I'd never met was cooler than I ever pictured her being.

Chapter Twelve

The mall was certainly a sensory overload. "Genie in a Bottle" blasted from speakers that practically shook the whole building. Packs of teens roamed around. I felt like a historian getting a glimpse into another world. It was sad to say but in the present time, it was rare to see that many kids hanging out together. Not only that but actually interacting with each other, rather than through their cell phones. People seemed to smile more, but maybe that was because the last twenty-five years hadn't weighed them down. 9/11 hadn't happened yet, or Trump and MAGA, the climate crisis. Now I understood what they meant when they said, "The good old days."

We went upstairs to the food court and sat at a round table eating Pizza Pizzazz. It was comforting that it tasted as good as it did in 2024. I always thought that their secret was sugar in the sauce. The music switched to "Hit Me Baby (One More Time)" and everyone went apeshit. Girls screamed like Britney Spears had entered the mall.

"It's certainly not Mozart," Kip said, taking a bite of pizza that yielded a long string of cheese.

"Oh, I'm sure people screamed just as much for him back in the day," Patty said.

"Are you defending Britney?" Maisie asked.

Patty tilted her head, as if in deep thought. "No, I mean, the music is trash, but I find Britney Spears to be empowering. Like she dresses how she wants. She's not afraid to be sexual."

Kip choked on his bite of pizza when Patty said the word "sexual," which I had to admit was not easy to hear coming out of your mom's mouth.

"I can see her as a role model for shy girls like me," Patty said, and looped a long strand of hair around her ear.

"Why be shy?" Simon asked. "Who cares what people think of you?"

"Maybe in Elgin it doesn't matter, but in Jeremiah Boonton, kids can be ruthless," Patty said. "I told you about the Britneys, calling me Cousin Itt, but it's happened since I was little."

Maisie reached across the table and patted Patty's hand. "We're not popular either. It's not good to peak in high school. I'm just getting started."

"Thanks," Patty said. "That's a good way to think of it."

Patty smiled, showing all of her teeth. I couldn't remember the last time I'd even seen her smile. A tear crinkled in my eye, but I refused to let it fall. In the future after we were successful, I'd be seeing my mom smile a million times over.

"So, Alex and Matthew, tell me more about yourself," Patty said, taking a sip of her Coke.

"I have a detective agency," I said. "In Elgin."

"A detective agency?" Patty said. "What kind of cases?"

"Usually missing cats and such, but there's a secret one I'm working on right now."

I could feel Simon's gaze, none too happy that I brought this up.

"Oooh," Patty said, rubbing her hands together. "Can you give us any hints?"

"It's super hush hush, but very important. Can't reveal any more out of respect."

Patty put her hand over her heart. "I totally understand. What about you, Matthew?"

Simon coughed into his napkin. "Uh, I'm an inventor."

Patty turned to Kip. "Kip, didn't you say you were an inventor too?"

Kip bit into his pizza. With too much cheese in his mouth, he couldn't respond. It didn't seem to be working out great between them. Patty appeared to be more interested in me and Simon.

"Hey," I said quietly to Simon, while poking him in the ribs. "Let's get Mom and Dad taking more."

"Affirmative," Simon said to me and then raised his voice. "My inventions are nothing compared to Kip." He chewed on his words, barely able to get them out.

"Kip, what are you working on?" Patty asked, as Dad still chewed his giant bite of pizza. He held a finger up as he swallowed, then started coughing. His face turned bright red and a vein bulged in his forehead. I prayed we wouldn't have to give him the Heimlich.

"Here, have a sip of my soda," Patty said, and passed it over.

Kip looked as if he questioned whether it was really okay, but Patty kept nodding. He took a few sips until he got his coughing under control.

The Britney Spears song ended and Blink 182's "What's My Age Again?" started playing. Maisie squealed to my surprise.

"I love this old song," Maisie said.

"Old?" Patty asked.

"Uh, dance with me, M—I mean, Alex."

Maisie reached out her hand and I got out of my seat to start dancing. I was a terrible dancer, never knowing what to do with my arms, so I wound up just flinging them around. Maisie sensed my nervousness and grabbed my arms to calm me down.

"Matthew, join us," Maisie shouted over the music.

Simon shook his head.

"Oh, come on," Maisie said and danced over to him. She brought him to his feet, and while Simon didn't dance, he at least took the hint not to sit back down.

"I wanted to give them a chance to be alone," Maisie said.

"Good thinking," Simon said, and I could swear I saw him tap his foot.

"I think it's going really well," I said, jumping around and singing, "*What the hell is wrong with me?*"

We looked over, but Kip and Patty weren't talking. She was spinning a strand of hair around her finger and he was glued to his pizza. Oof.

"Time for another plan," Maisie said, spinning away from us until Simon and I were left dancing by ourselves. Simon stopped tapping his foot and went back to the table. The song ended and I returned as well.

"This mall is lame," Maisie said. "What's your place like?"

"Mine?" Patty said.

"Yeah, why don't we hang there? It's not even six o'clock."

"Uh, I don't usually have guests over."

"All the more reason to have some!" Maisie said. "It's solved. Are you far?"

"No...we can walk."

"Great," Maisie said, and turned to give me and Simon a wink. The Backstreet Boys came up on the speakers and she frowned. "That way we can put on whatever music we want."

"Okay..." Patty said, tucking her hair behind her ear. It could tell it was what she did when she was nervous.

I wondered if it was because she was afraid her parents would be home.

And if things had already started getting bad between them.

Chapter Thirteen

When we opened the front door to Patty's house, we could already sense the tension. Her parents—my grandparents—were in mid-fight and stopped immediately when they saw us. An echo of a curse hung in the air. Grandma Lillian died when I was a little kid, and all I remembered of her was being a shriveled old thing with a cane she used to swat me with if she thought I was misbehaving. She lived on a soup diet, only frowned, and smelled of mothballs. Mom, however, doted on her. This was before Mom got catatonic of course. If Grandma Lil, or Grandma "Ill"— as Simon and I would call her behind her back—came over, Mom could do no right, despite doing everything for her. At Grandma Ill's funeral, when the coffin lowered, Mom said "Good."

It seemed like time had definitely affected the Grandma Ill I knew, since she looked more robust in this past and that she ate more than just soup. She had her hair in a bun and there was no moth smell. She wore a lot of makeup with rosy cheeks and lots of what I thought was eye shadow. A tiny little mouth that always looked like she was sucking on a lemon. Her vicious eyes locked on us with surprise.

My grandfather Scoot died a long time before I was born. After making life miserable for Grandma Ill and Mom, he left town never to be heard from again. About a year later, Ill and Mom got word that he had passed from a bad liver. They both chose not to go to the funeral, already considering him dead. His leaving had affected Ill the worst. She became lonely and bitter and vengeful with no one else to take it out on except for Mom. I felt a swirl of anger at him for causing our family so much pain. In my head, I imagined him to be more menacing, but he really wasn't. Slim with a bald moon on his head and wisps of hair. Big, expressive eyes and a long and winding nose. A mouth full of spittle. A stupid white lab coat on, which probably meant he just got home from work.

"Patty," he said, recoiling his hand. I wondered if he intended to hit Grandma Ill. "You've brought guests?"

The way he said it made me believe that Patty had never brought home guests before. It was sad that her life was so small, stuck with these losers.

"These are my friends," Patty said, curling a hair around her ear with her signature move. "This is Kip, Alex, Matthew and Maisie."

Scoot blinked in response, not even offering to shake our hands.

"Hello," Ill said, actually smiling—or giving as much of a smile as she could muster. She probably just wanted to get away from Scoot. "Welcome to our house." She swept her arm back to showcase the living room filled with a couch, a TV, and a painting of swans. She caught me looking at the swans.

"I love swans," she said, with a tear in her eye that she shook away.

"Who doesn't?" I said, because I couldn't think of anything else.

"Really?" she said, the veins in her neck protruding. "What do you love about them?"

"Uh…"

"Patty," Scoot said abruptly. "You really should have told us you were bringing guests. The house is a mess and we have no food to offer them."

"I'm sure I can scrounge something up," Ill said, pursing her lips.

"We ate at the mall," Maisie said. "Pizza Pizzazz."

"Your hands are filthy," Ill said to her, as Maisie gazed down.

"Oh, it's paint," Maisie said. "From even before we jumped."

She realized her mistake.

"I mean, can I use your bathroom?"

Scoot seemed like he didn't want to let Maisie anywhere near a bathroom, but nodded to his right. Maisie hung her head as she went down a hall.

"We'll go in my room, Daddy," Patty said. "We won't be a bother."

"Yes," Ill said, taking out a wet tissue from her pocket and blowing her nose. She was still trying not to cry. "Your father and I were discussing something important when you walked in."

Scoot glared at his wife, as if she wasn't allowed to speak. I just wanted to get the hell away from them.

"Yeah," I said, yanking at Patty. "Patty had a…a

CD she wanted to show us. "*No Scrubs*," I said, remembering the dance those girls did back in the parking lot when we first went to Congley's car.

We all scurried into Patty's room. Once the door closed, we could hear a muffled version of Scoot and Grandma Ill's fight. I heard the word "job," but couldn't make out more than that.

Patty's room was small. A rug in the center and a tiny twin bed. She had posters of George Michael and Debbie Gibson that had curled and appeared to be left over from when she was younger. The ceiling was covered in Glow-in-the-Dark stars and constellations. She walked over to a desk covered in homework papers and textbooks and turned on a Lava lamp.

"I'm sorry about them," she said, and sat on her bed. She reached over and pressed a button on a portable boombox until Janet Jackson came on. Janet drowned out their fighting enough.

"Parents always suck," I said to make her feel better and because it was really true. I looked over at Kip, who'd been absent as a dad because he had to take care of the future version of her.

"Not like mine," she said, rubbing her nose. "It's gotten worse. It's because of my dad's job."

Simon sat on the bed next to her. "What does your dad do?"

Patty looked surprised, since Simon hadn't spoken much this whole time. He was dead ass focused on the mission and nothing else.

"He owns a company. Nimo Industries. Named after himself obviously."

"What do they make?" Simon asked, as if he was interrogating a witness.

"I don't really know." She threw up her hands.

"Something science-y. It doesn't make much sense to me. All I know is he's been fighting with his business partner a lot."

Simon faced her. "Fighting about control of the company?"

"Yes." She cocked her head to the side. "How did you know?"

"That's usually what business partners fight about," Simon said, confident. "You can't let the partner get control of the company."

"Matthew…" I started to say, warning Simon to chill but he ignored me.

"Why do you care?" Patty asked. Scoot and Ill's fighting rose up a notch, so she turned up the music too.

"It's obviously affecting you," Simon said smoothly. "You're upset."

Patty frowned. "They fight *all* the time."

"Maybe we can help? I'm looking to do an… internship at a scientific institution. That would be perfect. Alex too."

"Me?" I said, my voice rising ten octaves. "I can't do science."

Simon brushed me away. "You're better than you think. I can ask your dad, Patty. It may even diffuse the fight with your mom."

Patty sighed, off in another world. "You could try."

"I will," Simon said, jumping up. "C'mon, Alex."

"What about Kip?" Patty said. "You're so smart too."

Kip was fiddling with a tiny unicorn that slipped out of his hands and broke. "Shit, sorry."

Patty shrugged. "It's ok. That's just a little kid's toy. I don't even know why I still have it."

"No," Simon said. "Kip, you stay here with Patty. We don't want to leave you alone."

"I'm fine—"

"No," Simon said, raising his voice so everyone jumped. "Sorry, it's just that he's not going to be open to the three of us doing an internship, that's too much. Sorry, Kip."

Kip tried to wedge the unicorn leg that had broken back in its hole. "I don't think I would have the time anyway."

"See?" Simon said. "Let me work my magic. C'mon, Alex."

I got up and Simon and I left her room, closing the door as Maisie returned from the bathroom. We could really hear Scoot and Ill going at it. Ill crying that Scoot has "changed," and Scoot demanding that he's "stressed beyond belief."

"Where are you guys going?" Maisie asked.

Simon walked past her. "I'm pitching our grandfather about Miles and I doing an internship at his company."

"What about me?" Maisie asked.

Simon spun around. "What about you? You are not my priority."

"Hey…Simon," I started to say.

"No, Miles, she's in the way. If she wants to help, go into the bedroom and work on getting our parents to like each other. Dad is so awkward I don't understand how Mom could've ever fallen for him."

"You don't have to be a dick," Maisie mumbled.

"I don't have time *not* to be a dick," Simon said, before swiveling back around and beckoning me to follow.

"I'm sorry, Maze," I said. "This is the mission."

Maisie gave me the finger. "Fuck your mission."

She burst into the bathroom as Janet Jackson's "That's the Way Love Goes" played before the door slammed in my face.

Chapter Fourteen

When Simon and I reached the living room, Scoot and Ill were really in the throes of a fight. Ill was crying, her face turned away. Scoot was cleaning up a lamp that had broken. Ill wrestled a tissue out of her sleeve and blew a foghorn. "You're impossible," she said to him, under her breath. "Just impossible." She looked up at us, embarrassed we'd see her in such disarray. "Oh, Patty's friends," she mumbled and blew into the tissue again.

"Sorry, can we help you clean?" Simon asked. I'd never seen him acting so polite before, but I knew he was just faking it to get in with Scoot.

"What?" Scoot asked, sweeping the lamp debris into a dustpan.

Simon picked up a cracked bulb. "Here."

Scoot took the bulb and dumped it all in a garbage bin. "Was there something you both needed?"

"Excuse me," Ill said, using the distraction to flee. She picked up her pace until she was gone down the hall.

Scoot gave the kind of a sigh that only a middle-aged man could, like the world was heavy.

"Patty said you work in sciences?" Simon asked.

Scoot stared as if he was dumbfounded to be in a conversation with us. "Yes, my company—we back innovations…in the science field."

"I'm an inventor," Simon said. "And science is my passion." He gave me a kick. "Both of us."

"Uh, yes," I said. "I leave and breathe everything science."

Simon glared at me. "Anyway, we're looking for internships. Our school in Elgin requires one, but you know Elgin…not much opportunity for anything."

Scoot managed a gruff laugh.

"Would you possibly have any openings at your company?" Simon asked, dialing up the charm to the max.

Scoot stared at where the lamp had broken, still probably stuck in the fight that occurred with Ill.

"We're really smart," I said. "Like, the smartest. And hard workers. If you give us a task, like that task is getting done."

"Right," Simon said, and then launched into a monologue with so much scientific jargon that it sounded like a different language. Scoot seemed to light up and the two of them continued what could only be described as an instant lovefest that had them laughing and shaking hands.

"Rare to meet such a fine mind at your age," Scoot said.

Simon gleamed. "I could say the same for you."

Ho, ho, ho, they both began to laugh again.

Scoot tapped his chin. "We could use an intern for

the new project we've started. It's been hitting a lot of snags."

"Consider me a snag eliminator," Simon said, and both of them roared until tears crinkled from their eyes.

"All right, could you come tomorrow?" Scoot asked. "My partner would have to approve, but since you'll be working for free, I can't see him saying no."

"Tomorrow would be great. And we can go on our internships during school hours. That's how it works in Elgin."

Scoot crossed his arms. "Really? That's odd."

"Our school is so bad, they encourage it. To give us a chance to learn something."

"Elgin," Scoot scoffed. "Full of folks whose elevators do *not* all go to the top floors."

"You'd be doing us a big solid," Simon said.

"Wait, *us*?" Scoot asked.

"Yeah," Simon said. "Me and my brother."

I gave a foolish wave.

Scoot scrunched up his face. "I'm not sure we could take on two interns."

"Well, Alex is smart," Simon said. "Smarter than me even, despite his youth."

"I'm gifted," I said.

Simon threw his arm around me. "We come as a package."

We heard a crash coming from down the hall. "Scoot?" the voice weakly said.

Scoot gave us an FML look. "Wives," he said, blowing a raspberry. "Can't live with 'em, can't kill 'em."

"What?" I said, making a face.

"I'm just—" Scoot blew into his cheeks. "Lillian

requires a lot. Between you and me, she doesn't understand the stressors of my job. The pressures of a scientific mind."

Scoot gestured for us to come closer. We obliged.

"See, it's *my* company. And when you're the boss, it's a constant battle with my underlings, even my partner who doesn't see things as I do."

"How so?" Simon asked.

"Well, my partner backs the money, but the company would be nothing without my mind. He thinks he has a similar kind of intelligence, but my talent can't be taught."

Simon nodded. "I feel exactly the same. That's why Alex and I need to get out of Elgin. The students and teachers are all simpletons."

"Yes," Scoot said, sucking on his teeth. "This could be good. Would you back me up if need be? My partner is always trying to undermine—"

"Of course," Simon said. "We could be your eyes and ears at the company."

Scoot was practically salivating. "And you'd report everything to me?"

"Scoot," Simon said, extending his hand. "You have our word."

We shook on it and he gave us the address for Nimo Industries tomorrow.

Down the hall, Ill started wailing again, but Scoot shook his head. "Not my problem right now," he said. "I'm taking a walk." Then he spun out of the door.

We headed down the hallway and found Ill quivering on the ground. She had fallen. We helped her up as an empty alcohol bottle fell from her pocket. From the wafting fumes, it looked as if it had been freshly opened and devoured.

"Oh," she said, and bent down to pick it up but changed her mind when she saw it was empty. "Looks like someone drank it all." She gazed up with glassy eyes. "I might... would you gentlemen take me to my bed? I think a nap is in order."

"Sure," I said. Simon took her arm on one side and I got the other. We brought her to her room and lay her down in bed, took off her shoes. She cried into the pillow like she'd lost someone she cared about, apologizing through her tears.

"My husband," she said. "My husband."

"He went for a walk," Simon said.

"He's cruel. I don't want to be like him," she said, as if she was helpless. "I fear I'm...becoming him."

I pulled the sheets up to her neck. "You don't have to."

"It might be too late. I have no one to...no one... who understands. And Patty, she gets me at my worst." She turned her head until she was speaking into her sopping pillow. "Can you look after her? I'm so glad she has friends."

"We will," I said, but Ill immediately started snoring.

We backed out and closed the door.

"She doesn't want to be bad," I said.

"But she is. She hurts Mom. We know this."

"Maybe we can save her too?"

"Don't be naïve, Miles. She's evil. She's making excuses."

"You saw how Scoot treats her."

"Doesn't mean she needs to take it out on Mom."

"No, but she's weak."

"No argument there."

"Anyway," Simon said. "She's not our priority here. Just like Maisie shouldn't be your priority either."

He walked past me and opened Patty's door as Janet Jackson still played, but this time it was the song "Scream," her duet with her brother Michael.

> *Stop pressuring me.*
> *You make me wanna scream.*

I could relate.

Chapter Fifteen

After leaving Mom's house, we went down to Generator Street where Congley built his underground lab. To make it easy to remember, he had "Nimo" be the password, just like it was at the lab in present time. Climbing down, I noticed how much more bare bones it was in 1999. When I was there in the present, the time machine had been built with a million computers flashing and beeping, but here Congley only had one, which he hunched over with a grimace.

When he saw us, he fixed the glasses up on his nose and we told him what happened. We successfully got to know the younger versions of both Mom and Dad and set up an internship for Simon and me at Nimo Industries. Simon and I were psyched, or at least as psyched as Simon would ever physically show, but Maisie seemed the opposite. She lay down on one of the thin mattresses in the corner that Congley had gotten for us. I went over but she turned her back to me.

"What's wrong?" I asked. I could hear Simon and Congley discussing scenarios about all they had to accomplish before we'd be able to return to the present.

"I'm worthless," Maisie said.

"C'mon."

She rolled over, her face stained with tears. "Like, there's no reason I should be in 1999. I hate everything about it. The music sucks and everyone seems too happy. They're all so delusional at how bad things are gonna get."

"That's true, but you're really helping us out."

"How?"

She had a point.

"And your brother hates me."

"He doesn't hate you."

"He's never been nice to me. I feel like I'm getting in the way. And I brought that horrible woman into this era. We don't even know what she'll try to do."

"I like to think that everything happens for a reason."

Maisie scoffed, choking on a ream of snot.

"No, Miles, there's no reason for me to be here."

I grabbed her hand. "You're here because I care and because…"

"What?"

I didn't know if I should tell her that we found out her mom worked for Omni and was sent back in time, never to reappear.

"There's something I haven't told you."

She sat up, giving me a look like she knew this wasn't gonna be good.

So, I told her everything. That Talia, her mom, was sent by a man named Horatio, the leader of Omni, back in time and she never returned. That she didn't just walk out on Maisie one day, and she might be in any era.

Maisie pulled at her hair. "Why didn't you tell me this before...?"

"I thought after this mission, we could travel through time to find your mom. I don't know where to start, but we could pinpoint—"

Maisie cut me off by punching me in the face. It wasn't hard, more of a way for her to get out some aggression. And I took it. Because I deserved it.

"How could you not tell me this, Miles?" she screamed. "For months. Like you knew how much it hurt me that I thought my mom just left. And now to find out that she's missing in time?"

Simon and Congley came over because they could hear us yelling.

Maisie jumped up and shoved Simon.

"And you," she said to him. "You probably told Miles not to say anything, so I wouldn't get in the way."

Congley got between them. "Let's not fight."

Maisie shoved him as well.

"Little girl," Congley said, stumbling back and putting on a tone. "If it's true you mother could be anywhere in time, there's no way for us to possibly know. While their mother—"

Maisie stomped her feet. "I know! It's all about *this* mission. And no one gives a fuck about me."

Congley twitched at Maisie's curse. "There's no need for language."

"Fuck you." She pointed her finger. "Fuck you, Simon, and you too, Miles. Whether the mom I knew is in this timeline or not, her younger self definitely is and I'm gonna find her."

I went to hug her but she pushed me away. "Where did she grow up?"

Maisie rubbed her forehead. "I don't even know. The Midwest. Somewhere in the Midwest. My brain isn't working."

I went to hug her again. This time, she didn't push me away as much.

"I wanna help you, Maze. And I'm gonna make a mission to find your mom. But this mission now—"

She wormed out of my arms. "I know, I know. Repeat things much? Like, I can't with your whininess right now, Miles."

"I'm not whiny," I said, but it did sound like a whine.

"I need space. Just…" She looked up at the trapdoor that led us down. She began to climb the ladder.

"Where are you going?" I asked.

"I don't know," she said. "Away from here."

She climbed to the top.

"Wait, Maisie…"

I went to go after her, but Simon stopped me.

"It's not worth it now," he said.

Maisie opened the trapdoor and scurried outside. She slammed down the trapdoor and was gone.

I felt the loss deep in the pit of my stomach, knowing it was all my fault for letting her go.

Chapter Sixteen

Maisie came back late last night after we had all gone to sleep and was gone before sunup. While I felt bad, it was nice not to have to worry about her getting along with Simon and having a purpose here. I hated to admit it, but I was regretting even telling her about the time machine. I'd never say this to Simon. He certainly didn't need an ego boost.

We headed out at dawn to Nimo Industries wanting to make a good impression. The building was located off Main Street down a twisty block with an ice cream store on the corner. Even this early, there were already kids waiting in line for a sugar high before class. I think I spotted the Britneys from after-school class, who all giggled from the sight of us.

I was pacing like I had to pee. "I'm nervous I won't understand any of the science stuff they'll say."

"Just mimic whatever comes out of my mouth," Simon said.

He hit the buzzer and the door opened to a woman with punk purple hair and a scowl.

"Yes?" she said, tapping her foot.

"We're here for the internship." Simon extended his hand, but she swiveled around, assuming we'd follow.

We headed down a metal hallway passing a few doors. The sounds of bleeps and bloops came from under the doorjamb. When we reached a large windowless room bathed in fluorescent lights, she left us alone without a word.

"What do you think they make here?" I asked.

Simon was glancing around. "We'll soon find out."

Scoot walked out of a door with a man who could only be described as grim. He was balding but had swept a large amount of hair from the back of his head over his forehead. It seemed to stay in place by only luck. His features were all small: tiny eyes, barely a nose, and thin lips that weren't really lips but more like two lines that settled on a frown. He had broad shoulders, a thick midsection, thin legs like toothpicks, and walked with a cane. He coughed into his hand and held it out.

"Ah, the interns. I'm Mr. Thoorai."

His hand remained covered with the tiniest trace of spittle. I prayed Simon would shake it first, but he had the same idea as me so I gave in, the spittle warm against my palm.

"Alex," I said. "Thanks so much for the opportunity."

"Hrmph," he said, shoving his hand at Simon. When he shook, Mr. Thoorai made sure he was in charge.

"Both kids have a great mind," Scoot said, although he appeared distracted.

Mr. Thoorai stuck his hands in his pockets. "I'll be the judge of that. Quick, what is the square root of fifty-six thousand, seven hundred and seventy-five?"

Simon's lips spun as he worked the equation in his head. "Two hundred thirty-eight point two seventy-five, etcetera, etcetera."

Mr. Thoorai did not seem impressed.

"That's an easy one," he sneered, his nostrils flaring that made him look piggish.

He bared his teeth that slid up his gumline. "What is the Mpemba effect?"

Simon gave a smirk. "Why hot water freezes faster than cold water. The theory is that hot water is less dense and evaporates more, which causes it to cool faster. Another theory is that hotter systems of matter may reach equilibrium—"

"What about your sidekick?" Mr. Thoorai barked. "Does he talk?"

"He's shy," Simon said.

"No room for shy wallflowers here." He stood over me, his eyes running up and down, not enthralled with what they saw. "Roughly how long does it take the sun's light to reach the earth: eight minutes, eight hours, or eight days?"

"Uh…" I glanced at Simon.

"Don't look at him," Mr. Thoorai snapped, rapping his cane against the floor.

"M-u-s-i…" Simon said, masking a cough. He was smart enough to use the Okoboji language that we created when we were kids. In Okoboji, only the third letter of every word counted.

"Minutes," I said, confident.

"Lucky guess," Mr. Thoorai said, bidding us away.

He turned around and slammed his cane into the floor as he walked out.

We were taken to a room off the side where the bleeps and bloops came from. Machines that looked like film reels spun while they flashed different colors.

"Irma will brief you," Mr. Thoorai said, and then slammed the door.

We were left confused when the door opened again and Scoot stuck his head inside.

"Excuse him," Scoot said. "He has no social skills. If you're not getting yelled at, consider it a lucky day."

"He didn't seem to be too excited to have us here," I said.

Scoot gritted his teeth. "Excitement isn't in his vocabulary."

"So, what are we doing here exactly?" Simon asked.

Scoot wiggled his ears and made his eyes big. "My eyes and ears, remember?" He peered down the hall. "In case you hear anything negative about me, report it back."

"Right," Simon said. "But that's not all—"

"Irma will brief you," Scoot said. "At the end of each day, I'll have you clue me in on anything suspicious."

I raised my hand. "Like….?"

Scoot frowned. "Like anything suspicious. Obviously. This isn't rocket science…" He searched for my name and I almost said Miles.

"Alex."

He slapped his forehead. "Right, Alex. And Matthew." He lowered his voice. "The truth is they are looking for anything to squeeze me out."

"Who is *they*?" Simon asked.

Scoot genuinely looked spooked. "All of them. Shit, she's coming."

Before we could say anything, he whisked down the hall.

The purple-haired lady arrived in his place. She seemed familiar, possibly someone who had stayed in town all these years that I recognized, but I couldn't figure it out. Since it would be twenty-five years later, I imagined her old. Working at the library. Or the yarn store. Behind her, she tugged a cart filled with stacks of paper.

She picked up a heft of papers and slammed it down on a desk.

"See these papers?" she asked. "They are filled with numbers. Ones and zeros. Circle the ones, underline the zeros."

I could sense Simon fuming. "That's it?"

She put her hand on her hip. "That's it."

"So, what are we doing here?" I asked, but she'd already stepped out of the door, shutting it behind her. "This place is weird."

"That's stating the obvious."

He grabbed a piece of paper and started circling and underlining. "They're giving us busy work."

I slid a piece of paper from the top and stared down at a million ones and zeros that looked like a nightmare. "I'm gonna barf."

Simon fixed his glasses. "You're not going to barf. Do the work quickly, so we could then snoop."

"Snoop on Scoot?"

"Precisely."

"The mission is for him not to get pushed out of the company. At whatever cost."

"I know, I know…"

"But we can't change too much. You know a butterfly flaps his wings—"

"And makes a typhoon."

"It's not quite as simple as that. Time. Everything that was meant to happen has already happened."

I scratched my head. "What do you mean?"

Simon cleared his throat. "There is no past or present or future. It is all one. So, if we change something in 1999, it shouldn't affect 2024 because we were always going to change it in 1999."

"Okay, so who cares about the butterfly effect then?"

"This is where it's tricky. You can't change things on a grand scale. Life or death. If someone dies in 1999, who was meant to be alive in 2024…"

"Doesn't it mean they were always supposed to die?"

"Not quite. Because they were alive in our original version of 2024."

"Ugh, my head hurts."

"Small changes. Like, fixing Mom. Just not preventing 9/11, or Trump becoming president. Like, we can't kill baby Hitler."

"Baby Hitler, what are you talking about?"

"You can't kill baby Hitler because maybe killing him would cause an even worse demagog to rise."

"I'm gonna refrain from killing anyone."

Simon winked. "That's the spirit."

The door swung open, causing us both to jump.

Irma stood there scowling. "How much have you finished?"

"Have we finished this massive stack of papers in like two seconds?" I asked.

"Go faster," she said, shutting the door.

"I hate this place already," I said.

Simon was scribbling fast. He had already finished quadruple the amount of papers as me.

"You are slow, Miles."

"F off," I said, staring down as the ones and zeros swirled.

Chapter Seventeen

I was exhausted after a full day at Nimo Industries. When I got back, all I wanted to do was sleep. I was sure Simon did as well, but he and Mr. Congley had to do tests on the time machine glove. Simon knew exactly how to build it; the difficulty was getting all the parts he needed in 1999. So far, there were a few things Congley was having a hard time finding.

Just as I was about to take a nap on a mattress in the corner, Maisie returned. She climbed down the ladders and landed with a jump, stirring me from whatever sleep I tried to enter.

"Hey," I said, rubbing my eyes. "How was your day?"

She tapped her chin. "Hmmm, how was my day? While dealing with the trauma of learning my mother could be alive in some timeline, I did manage to check out the town."

She took a sip from a Snapple raspberry iced tea.

"This is soooo gooood by the way. I know they

have it in the present, but not like this. I think there's more sugar. They're fucking with our sugar, Miles!"

"Who? Are you drunk?"

Maisie grinned. "Oh no, I'm stoned."

"What? Who did you smoke with?"

"Are you my keeper? Like, if I want to smoke pot, I don't need your permission."

"No, but…"

"But nothing." She drained the Snapple, tossed it in the garbage, and belched. "Some guy named Len. He's an artist."

From the way she said it, she was rubbing in the fact that I couldn't draw for shit.

"He was wearing JNCOs. Those are like really huge jeans. Honestly, they would be really popular now. I met him because there's an art show happening in town and anyone could join. The winner gets a thousand dollars. Like, I could buy a plane ticket to wherever my mom grew up."

"Why do you wanna see your mom in this timeline?"

Maisie yelled, "Because I miss her. Here you and Simon get to see *both* of your parents and form new memories of them. And I just miss her. All right? I do."

"She wouldn't be your mom like you know. She'd be a teenager."

"I'm aware of that, thank you very much. So, I saw some of the art that had already been entered and I could beat it. I can."

"Cool, I think you should then."

She mimicked me. Then maybe felt bad because she made a face. "I don't want to fight with you, Miles."

I breathed a sigh. "I don't want to fight with you either."

She opened up her shirt and brushes and paint fell to the floor.

"Where'd you get that?"

She shrugged. "Len and I stole it after we smoked one of his blunts."

I wanted to yell at her for being so careless, but kept my mouth shut. She wasn't angry at me anymore, at least while she was high. I wanted to keep it that way.

"What does Len do?"

Maisie started organizing her paint on a table. "He's older. A senior. Well, he dropped out, got his GED."

"Sounds like a dream."

"Please, you would be into him," she said.

"What's that supposed to mean?" I asked, a little hurt that she was taking a dig at me being bi. Especially since she was bi too.

"Forget it." She put on a smile that had to be fake. "How was your day?"

Simon walked back in the room grumbling and went to the mini fridge, pulling out a bottle of Clearly Canadian soda.

"The day was insufficient," he said, cooling his forehead with the drink after taking a sip. "I'm still missing some parts for the glove."

"Might we be stuck in this time?" Maisie asked, and from the way it sounded, it seemed like she didn't care.

"Negative," he said. "I'll find the parts. The bigger problem is making inroads at Nimo Industries. Mr. Thoorai just had us doing busy work the whole time."

"Nimo Industries?" Maisie asked. "That's the name of it?"

"Yeah, after Scoot's last name," I said.

She laughed. It honestly felt good to hear, since she'd been mostly upset since we arrived.

"What's so funny?" Simon asked.

"Rearrange the letters. N.I.M.O. C'mon, can't you see it?"

Simon slapped his head. "Omni!"

"Duh," Maisie said. "Some genius you are."

"We've been busy," Simon gasped. "I just didn't have a chance to…"

Maisie put her hand on her hip. "How about a thank you?"

"Thank you," Simon said.

"Omni!" I squealed. "So, Scoot is the original founder of Omni?"

Simon snapped his fingers. "Before it was taken over by that guy Horatio we heard them talking about in our time."

"Wait," Maisie said. She opened a red paint jar and dipped in a brush. Then she wrote out the name Horatio on the floor. "What was the name of the boss there, Simon?"

"Thoorai. Mr. Thoorai?"

She painted the name Thoorai on the floor and we all saw what it meant.

I said it out loud.

"Thoorai is an anagram for Horatio."

———

After we all got over the shock of it, Simon spoke about how it made perfect sense. This town was too small to have any other big company springing up at this time besides Omni. All we knew from the present time was that the head of it was named Horatio, and we shut it down, since Maisie's father Smith blew up the place after he'd got caught. Obviously, he torched it to get rid of any evidence. We didn't hear about Omni resurfacing anywhere else and hadn't been threatened by Horatio, but it had only been six months, so it was likely that they were plotting how to come back even bigger and more menacing than before.

Simon looked at his watch. "We should go to the physics group, since school will be ending."

I'd completely forgotten about it, too swept away from what we just learned.

"Hold on," I said, a chill licking down my spine. "You don't think…that woman Irma with the purple hair. Do you think she's the spikey-haired woman who jumped back with us?"

Simon nodded. "Could very well be. Which means the spikey-haired woman would likely be headed there."

"From what we know," I said. "Running to yourself in the past doesn't break the time-space continuum."

"No," Simon said. "But there's got to be a way to use this to our advantage. Let's go to the after-school class. We can run scenarios while getting closer to Mom and Dad."

"Count me out," Maisie said. "I'm gonna paint."

"You sure you'll be okay—" I began, but she cut me off.

"Here in this basement of a silo with Mr. Congley next door. Yeah, I think I'll survive."

"Thank you again for figuring out Omni," I said,

feeling worms in my stomach from treating Maisie like she didn't matter. "I knew it was important for you to be in 1999."

"Oh, did you?" she said, sarcastically as ever. She was still mad.

"Yeah, anyway. I'm sorry." I kicked Simon, who was standing next to me.

Simon looked at the floor. "Yes, sorry too. You've really helped us out."

Maisie beamed, but it had to be fake. "You're welcome. Both of you. I'm glad this dumb girl could be of such assistance."

I went to respond, but she'd taken out a sheet of paper to paint on and wouldn't look in my direction.

"C'mon, Miles," Simon said, yanking me.

So, I left Maisie alone and followed.

Chapter Eighteen

At the after-school class, we were passed a spiral journal that said BFF or More? The Britneys all giggled when I opened it. I saw my name—well, Alex —along with a chart that said BFF or More? All the Britneys wrote More! and one even circled my name with a heart. I gulped. I turned the page and saw Simon—well, Matthew—with the same quiz. All the girls wrote More, as well. I guessed Simon and I were hot commodities in 1999.

I showed him but he couldn't care less, too focused on figuring out the next steps with Omni. The quandary, to use his words, was even if we managed to prevent Scoot from getting kicked out of his company, that could set off a chain reaction to make Omni even more powerful. We'd defeated Horatio's version of Omni in 2024, but we might not be successful with Scoot's. It all made my head hurt.

Patty spied the BFF book and whispered, "Looks like you've made some friends?"

We glanced over at the Britneys, who all wore

belly-bearing shirts with Doc Martin sliders. They gave a sea of waves.

"Not my type," I said.

Patty curled her long hair around her ear. "What's your type then?"

Ruh-roh. Was my mom hitting on me? I had to steer this in another way.

"I'm like…" I lowered my voice even more. "I'm bi."

"Oh," Patty said, jerking back. "I mean—I didn't know."

Was I coming out to my mom right now?

"I didn't either," I said. "Well, I guess I always thought—I just like both. It's different with guys than it is with girls. It's hard to describe."

She smiled. "No, I think that's really cool. That you know who you are."

My shoulders relaxed. "Thank you. I always say, it's just a small part me, not everything. Like, it doesn't have to be. And Maisie and I—we're a thing."

"Yeah, I figured."

"But we've been fighting, between you and me."

"What about?" She put her hand on mine. "You can tell me anything, Alex."

"Maybe…uh…back at your place. Like, not in public."

She blew her hair from her face. "You really wanna hang at my place? With my parents acting the way they do?"

"I wanna get to know you better. Become closer friends."

She petted her arm. "It's toxic at my home."

"I saw them yelling—"

She shook her head. "No, you don't even know.

Come," she said, getting up and taking my hand. "Not in public."

I locked eyes with Mr. Congley as me and Patty left the room and he gave me a nod. We reconvened near the bathroom. At this time of the day, no one was around. A janitor was mopping up a spill down the hall. I could hear his faint radio playing the Dave Matthews Band. When I looked up, Patty was in tears.

"Hey, don't cry."

She ran her sleeve across her eyes. "Thank you for sharing something so personal about you. I hope I… I'm sorry if I reacted shocked at first. I don't know too many other kids who are bi."

"It's okay. I guess in 1999, it's not as common."

She sniffed. "What do you mean by that?"

Shit.

"Oh…uh… Just that one day it probably won't be as big a deal."

She took a deep breath. "I have to tell you something too."

"Yeah, anything."

She rolled up her sleeve. A huge black and blue bruise ran from her wrist almost to her elbow.

"Holy shit, Patty, how did you—?"

She put her hand over my mouth. "Quiet."

We looked over at the janitor, who was still mopping to "Crash Into Me."

She took another deep breath from way, way down. "I told you about my dad—you've worked at his company now. You see how cutthroat it is."

"It's a strange place all right."

"So, he's getting pushed out. He put everything into this company. It's his life. Not just his life but mine and my mom's too."

"Did he hurt…?"

She raised her eyes, carefully, then shook her head.

"No, my mom did."

"How could she…?"

"Because he does it to her," Patty said, raising her voice. Finally, the janitor stopped whistling "Crash Into Me."

Lost for you I'm so lost for you…

Patty, my mom, just broke my heart.

"You can't let her do this," I said, wanting to run right down to her house and do the same to Grandma Ill. Call the cops on both my grandparents and save Patty from their abuse.

"It's complicated." Patty threw up her hands. "She drinks a lot. Like, a lot, a lot. She doesn't know what she's doing. And I've seen these kind of bruises on her."

"Doesn't make it okay."

"No, I'm not—*he's* the problem, my dad. But he's not, it's his job."

"It's just a job."

"It's not *just* a job."

"What do you…?"

"I overheard what they're trying to build there."

I froze, my guts squishing.

"A time machine."

━━

This time, I grabbed Patty's hand and yanked her away. I couldn't have the Dave Matthews crooning janitor hear about a time machine. We dashed into the library, surrounded by books, which put me at ease.

"A time machine?" I asked, pretending like it was the wildest thing in the world.

Patty grabbed a book from the shelf, H.G. Wells.

"Apropos," she said.

"You don't believe…?"

She flipped through the book, then tossed it aside. "No. I mean, I don't know. Dad's company has backed a lot of inventions before, but I've never seen them to be successful. I heard him talking on the phone to his business partner, Mr. Thoorai."

"Yeah, weird guy."

"The weirdest. Like, he gives me the chills. Always has. Even when I was little girl."

"They've known each other that long?"

"They grew up together. Except Mr. Thoorai was a bully. Dad said it was easier to just be friends with him. You know, keep your enemies close."

"One hundred."

"What?"

"Oh, like, a hundred percent. Definitely."

"You speak strange in Elgin."

"Yeah, we do. So…Mr. Thoorai wants the company to himself?"

"I believe that because they're getting close with the time machine, he wants to push my dad out. Which has been causing him to take it out on my mom, which causes her…" She rubbed her arm. "Anyway, I can handle it."

"Listen to me," I said, grabbing her by the shoulders. "Neither of your parents should be treating you this way. It's so *not* okay. You deserve better."

"They're all I got."

"No," I said, raising my voice. "They are not gonna do this to you again. Drag you down with them." I looked at her bruise. "Have you gone to the nurse?"

"I can't. She'll tell my parents and that'll make it worse."

"What about some CBD lotion?"

"What the hell is that?"

"Right, forget it. I wanna get you out of that house."

"Well, unless you have a place for me to stay, I'm stuck."

I thought of Congley's lab, but there was no way she could know about that.

"I'll figure something out."

She gave me a big hug. It felt—well, it just felt so damn good that I didn't want to let go. My mom hadn't hugged me since I was so little, a real hug, one with life behind it, behind her eyes. So we stood there hugging each other for different reasons surrounded by books and both of us unwilling to let go.

I could have stayed there for hours.

But eventually the janitor came by and we headed back to the room.

"Thank you," Patty said, just before we stepped inside.

I wanted to thank her more. "Of course, I'm here for you."

"I've never really had a friend. That sounds so bizarre to say. But it's true. Like, a real friend. Someone who cares."

I struggled with a lump in my throat. "I care."

"I know you do. And it means a lot. Because I care too."

She put her head on my shoulder. I found myself running my fingers through her hair when I saw a bald

spot, looking like she'd torn a tuft of hair out of anger,
or sadness, or to feel the pain of something other than
her life.

"I'm saving you," I whispered into that bald spot.

I didn't want her to hear, just to know that I was
here and I'd never give up until she'd be happy.

Her ear twitched, as if it picked up what I said.

I wasn't sure if she could possibly understand what
I meant.

Chapter Nineteen

At Nimo the next morning, I filled Simon in about our mom mentioning that Scoot was creating a time machine. We were put in the same room with stacks and stacks of papers. I could see ones and zeros behind my eyes, even when I closed them. Simon didn't answer at first. After the physics group when we got back to the underground lab, he and Congley went to work on building a glove to take us back to the present. I guessed a part they ordered had come in. I wanted to tell him about Mom then, but he and Congley shut the door, not wanting to be bothered. Even after I decided I'd tell Maisie, just to share it with someone, she wasn't home. Busy with her art competition and that guy Len. I hated Len already.

"Miles," Simon said, under his breath. "Pay attention."

He nodded up at a circular camera in the corner of the ceiling. Its buzz making the hairs on my arm stand.

"*They* are watching," he said, and then even quieter. "And probably listening."

"Okoboji?" I asked.

He gave a careful nod.

So we continued the conversation in the Okoboji language we'd created, where only every third letter in each word counted.

"Mom definitively said that her father is building a time machine?" Simon asked.

"She overheard him on the phone with Mr. Thoorai."

"Do you think she believes it's true?"

"I think she thinks *they* believe it's true. None of their inventions have been a success yet."

"Good." His lips pressed together in a way I didn't buy it.

"What, Simon?"

"We don't want her suspicious of us."

"She'd never guess she'd be hanging out with her future sons."

"She's smarter than you think. This isn't the mom of our present time."

"I came out to her. Like, told her I was bi."

"Oh," he said, taking off his glasses. "I'm listening."

Simon rarely ever listened, unless it was of course about time.

"She took it really well," I said. "She was cool."

"Good," he said. "I'm glad for you."

He gave me a pat on the shoulder, about the most affection I could expect from Simon.

"So, the plan for today," he said, entering into business mode. "We snoop around and look for the time

machine. Knowledge is power and if we have knowledge of it, we have power over them."

"To do what?"

"Neutralize Mr. Thoorai."

I rubbed my forehead. "I don't know what that
means."

He put back on his glasses, annoyed again. "Miles,
neutered. Like a dog. Mr. Thoorai wants Scoot removed
from the company, we have to flip it and get Mr. Thoorai."

I felt like I had to go to the bathroom. "Get him?
Like how?"

"To be determined."

"I don't like how you said that. You mean, kill
him?"

Simon slammed his fist. "Miles, you can only plan
so much. Variables arise. Congley and I were running
scenarios last night. If Mr. Thoorai is eliminated, that
chain reaction will save mom."

I raised my hand like I was asking a teacher a question. "What if it creates a worse chain and Mom is
even more out-to-lunch?"

"That is a variable. We can't know for sure, but
we've come to the past to take a chance. Think about
it, if Mr. Thoorai, or Horatio is out of the picture,
then we don't have a threat in the present."

"Unless Omni is always the treat and Mr. Thoorai
is a like a...what do you call it?"

"A figurehead."

"No, that doesn't sound right."

"Yes, Miles, it's a figurehead. Did you take dumb
pills today?"

"I'm finding I'm zoning out more..."

He looked at me funny. "You're bleeding."

"What?" I touched my nose. "Shit."

I grabbed one of the papers with ones and zeros as the door opened and Irma stepped in with her big head of purple hair. Her face still looked like it was trying to juice a lemon. She went to speak but then noticed the inordinate amount of blood gushing from my nose.

"What in the H. Christ is happening here?"

"I get bloody noses," I said, and then kicked myself.

Her eyes narrowed. Did she already know bloody noses were caused by time travel?

"Don't clean it up with the documents."

She yanked the bloody paper from my hand and pulled me out of the room. We went down a long, white hallway until we reached a bathroom.

"You have five minutes," she said, then looked down at her watch.

"Cool."

Inside the bathroom, fluorescent lights glared. I went to the mirror and splashed water on my face. A toilet flushed. Out stepped a guy in a lab coat. He was maybe a year or two older than me with black hair parted down the middle and frosted tips. He looked like a Backstreet Boy, but not one specifically. More like if you mushed them all together. Nick's hair. Brian's face. Kevin's body. Not that I really listened to the Backstreet Boys, all for 1999 research of course.

"Hey," he said and gave a salute on his way to the sink. "Wouldn't want to see the other guy?"

"What?"

He pointed at my nose. "The other guy. In the fight. Hope you socked him good."

He smiled a braces smile. It was weird to see

someone with metal braces, but it also kind of turned me on.

"Oh yeah, laid him out." I laughed. "Like, he's dead."

"Shit. Epic."

"So…epic."

"I'm Doug," he said, pointing to his name tag and offered his hand, then declined. "Actually, maybe you should clean up first."

"Total."

I grabbed a paper towel and made myself semi-presentable. "I'm Alex."

"Intern?"

"Yeah, me and my brother Simon started yesterday. Lots of ones and zeros."

"Oh, tell me about it. I remember those days."

"You actually work here now? As a job?"

"Yeah, it's a thing juniors can do at Boonton. Didn't recognize you…?"

"No, I go to Elgin."

He rolled his eyes. "Elgin? Wow, what a shit hole."

"Yeah, it kind of is."

"So, how you liking Nimo?"

I wasn't sure how much to reveal. "It's a…strange place to say the least."

He turned on the faucet and started washing his hands. "That's an understatement."

I relaxed in the fact that I could talk shit with Doug.

"I'm being monitored outside by the lady with the purple hair." I pointed toward the door. "She gave me five minutes off from my never-ending stack of papers."

"Irma?" He turned off the faucet. "She's a little SS in the way she watches."

"SS?"

"Like the Third Reich, just a joke." He flashed his braces smile. "She treats all the interns that way, so don't think you're special."

"What does she do here?"

Doug began whistling. "What do any of us do? Kidding again. She's Mr. Thoorai's right-hand man, er, woman."

More evidence that she'd eventually become the spikey-haired woman in the present.

"And Mr. Thoorai…?" I asked, leaving the question hanging.

Doug's eyes batted back and forth. An air vent sputtered over by the window. Doug clocked it, rather suspiciously. Doug put a finger to his lips.

"We don't speak ill of Mr. Thoorai here."

"No, I wasn't…"

He got in my face, his eyes bugging. "I said, we *don't* speak ill of Mr. Thoorai."

I gulped a breath. "Sorry, I…didn't mean."

Doug slapped his knee, cackling. "You should've seen your face. Kidding. Mr. Thoorai is like any boss, large and in charge."

"Oh, yeah, I knew you were kidding."

Doug shook his head. "No, I got you." His braces gleamed and then his mouth closed. "But it's never a good idea to talk smack about the boss."

"Right, right, sure."

He pulled a paper towel from the dispenser and dried his hands. "Alex, the intern. Wouldn't want to start off poorly here."

He went to walk past me, his shoulder lightly tapping mine.

"We should hang out," he said. "You like music?"

I was caught off guard. "Oh yeah…of course."

"I just bought a ton of CDs at Sam Goody. Wanna listen?"

I wondered if Doug might be more forthcoming about what it was like at Nimo outside of its walls. Or if he was coming on to me? I was always so clueless.

"That sounds awesome."

"It does sound awesome," he said. I couldn't tell if he was making fun of me, or whether Doug was the kind of guy who just liked to kid around.

"I'll meet you out front when the whistle blows," he said, firing a pretend finger gun at me.

"Toot toot," I said, and then immediately wanted to take it back.

His brow furrowed. "Okay, Alex, see you later."

I cringed as he left for acting so dorky. But I couldn't help it. I gave one last glance in the mirror to check if any blood remained and then exited too. Irma waited outside. She was on a giant cell phone with an antenna. She ended the call when she saw me.

"Took long enough," she said, and started walking.

I followed. "Sorry, I met Doug, who works here."

"Yes, I know he works here. We discourage fraternization among employees."

"Of course."

She led me back to the room where I could see Simon had made a dent in the stack of papers.

"Get back to work," she said.

"Ones and zeros await."

I gave her a heil salute as she grumbled, spun

around, and walked down the hallway, her boots firing into the floor.

"I think she's starting to like me," I said to Simon.

Chapter Twenty

Congley had found bikes for Simon and I to get around town, so I waited by the bike rack outside of Nimo for Doug. The rest of the day was uneventful. We tried to sneak out and find more about the time machine, but Irma kept a strict watch over us. Every time we exited the room to get a break from ones and zeros, she was in the hallway. We had to make excuses about our weak bladders, but even then, she'd monitor us and stand outside of the bathroom. So, we put our heads down and did as much work as possible. At least then, we'd be in good graces with her.

Simon was all for me going to Doug's to glean more info about Nimo. He said he'd handle Mom and Dad at the after-school program today and work on getting them closer together. Maybe the more time they'd spend with each other, the less that Patty would have to be in her abusive home. I still wanted to go over there and give Scoot and Grandma Ill a taste of their own medicine, but he warned me not to be impulsive. It was hard to even look at Scoot that day and play nice.

"Hey, Alex," Doug said as he left the building. He'd taken off his lab coat and was wearing a striped rugby shirt with baggy jeans and a puka shell necklace. "Follow me."

We hopped on our bikes and pedaled to his place. What was crazy—we zoomed right past *my* house. I slowed to take it all in. The front lawn where me and Simon used to hitch a tent and camp out under the stars when we were little. The screen door that I once snapped open too fast and broke a tooth. The window that led to my bedroom.

"C'mon, slowpoke," Doug said, since I was lagging behind, so I picked up the pace.

We reached Doug's house only a few blocks away. Pretty similar to my own. A picket fence and a manicured lawn.

"My parents aren't home," he said. "They work late. And my older brother is always out. He's a popular guy."

"Cool."

We entered to a living room with a fireplace and a small TV. On the mantel above were pictures of the family. Doug as a little kid with buck teeth. His older brother, a jock holding a football. Parents that looked as if they were most comfortable sitting in a church pew. Blond hair like helmets and big crosses hanging from their necks.

"I'm upstairs."

We headed past an old dog that responded with a sigh and went to Doug's room. I didn't know what I expected but when he opened the door, I was surprised. A huge poster of the band Creed hung on the wall. Another one of the movie, *The Crow*. The room was dark, the shades pulled down. The smell of socks hung in the air—the culprit a few stray pairs scattered on the floor.

"Mi casa es su casa," he said, flopping down on his messy bed and chewing some grape Bubble Tape. He picked up a guitar and noodled a few notes before putting it down.

I sat down at his desk in front of a large computer. "Not what I expected."

He made a face. "What did you expect?"

"I dunno." I shrugged. "Lighter, not as dark. Less…Creed."

He smacked his forehead. "You don't like Creed? They're the best."

He took out a CD case filled with hundreds of CDs. "This is my holy grail. Years of collecting." He passed it over to me as I flipped through. A lot of grunge music. Pearl Jam. Nirvana. Leading to Creed, 3 Doors Down, Korn, even Limp Bizkit.

"Limp Bizkit?" I said, taking out the CD and holding it like a dirty diaper.

Doug winked. "I did it all for the nookie. Do you do it all for the nookie, Alex?"

He whipped the CD from my hands and put it on as we listened to Fred Durst declaring that he did it all for the nookie too.

"Wouldn't have thought you were into this kind of music?" I shouted over the tortuous music.

"Oh yeah? How come?"

"Just with your hair." I pointed to the frosted tips. "Figured the Backstreet Boys were more your thing."

He gave me a leering look. "No. No way. They suck. That music is so gay."

I couldn't believe he'd say something so offensive, but then I remembered I was in 1999 and most kids probably spoke that way.

He glanced in the mirror. "Besides, my hair is cool. Like every dude has frosted tips in my class. Maybe it hasn't made it to Elgin yet."

"Probably." Limp Bizkit was grating my ears. "Can we put on something else?"

"Sure." He took out the CD and replaced it with "Higher" by Creed. He picked back up the guitar and began crooning along.

"Can you take me higher?" he sang. "Speaking of which."

He went to a drawer and removed a tiny box, opening it and taking out a pipe and a baggie of weed. "Let's get high."

"Oh, I don't…" I said, but he shook his head.

"No, man, we are getting super high. Won't take no for an answer."

He packed the pipe, lit it, and inhaled. Even blew a smoke ring. This guy was a pro, and I had to admit, I wanted to impress him.

"How was the rest of your workday?" I asked.

"I don't want to talk about that. I wanna take you higher."

Doug laughed into his fist and pushed the pipe in my direction. It was starting to feel like an Afterschool Special. I didn't want to come off like some inexperienced dork, so I took the pipe and inhaled. Immediately, I coughed out a ream of smoke. I couldn't stop coughing. I looked in the mirror and my eyes were bloodshot. I'd drank before, but never got high. Not that I was a prude or anything. It just hadn't happened yet.

"That was a good pull, man," Doug said, taking the pipe back for another big hit. "I love getting stoned. It was stressful today."

He leaned back against the headboard and kicked his Reebok Pumps off. He had a hole in his sock, his big toe sticking out and wiggling.

"I imagine Nimo can be stressful," I said. "I can't see straight after circling so many ones and zeros."

He blew a raspberry, then took another puff. "Nah, that's baby stuff. Not really what's important at Nimo."

I gulped. "What's important."

He giggled. "No, man, it's top secret. I can't spill."

I stood up and went over to the bed, took the pipe from him. "Anything I can do to convince you?" I pulled on the pipe, trying to be cool, but just started hacking again.

"Not a pro at smoking, huh?"

The Creed song ended. He reached over and flipped through his CD cases.

"What do you wanna hear next?"

He handed it to me. I kept flipping until I saw what looked like two CDs in a sleeve, one hidden behind the other.

"What's this?"

"Oh shit," he said, reaching to grab it back but I pulled out the CD from behind the other. Backstreet Boys *Millennium*.

"Backstreet Boys, huh?" I said.

He turned red. "Okay, okay. Like, I secretly like them, but would never admit it out loud. My brother would beat the shit out of me for playing them."

"Seriously? He'd beat you up?"

Doug nodded. "He has before. He'd call me a fa —" He bit his lip, then tossed his frosted bangs from his eyes. "Even the hair he made fun of. But I like it. Girls seem to like it."

I went over to the CD player with the Backstreet Boys CD.

"Alex, don't put that on."

"Your brother is not here."

I took out the Creed CD, swapping it with the Backstreet Boys and hit play. "I Want It That Way," came on. I'd heard this song before. Even in 2024, it was popular in a nostalgic way. But I knew back in 1999, you couldn't escape the song.

You are, my fire.

Doug leaped up from the bed and tackled me to the ground.

My one desire.

We wrestled around on the floor. He was bigger and stronger than me and pinned me down, both of us breathing heavy. With my arms over my head, he leaned down and planted a kiss on my lips. Then spun away. He got up and lowered the music, but didn't turn it off.

I was too high to react. Doug flopped down on his bed and picked up his guitar.

"But we are two worlds apart, can't reach to your heart," he sang, then tossed his guitar to the side. "Why'd you kiss me, man?"

My heart stopped. "You kissed me!"

He chuckled. "Unlikely. I'm not like…you know."

I crossed my arms. "Well, I'm bi. It's no big deal. And I have a…"

Shit, I completely forgot about Maisie. I couldn't believe I cheated on her! Well, I didn't really cheat on her, since Doug kissed me. Or maybe I did initiate it and was too high to realize.

"I have a girlfriend," I said. "Maisie."

"Yeah, I do too," Doug said. "She's a hot piece."

I made a face. "A hot piece?"

Doug raised an eyebrow. "What she don't know...?"

He stood up, stalking toward me with intent.

I want it that way, the Backstreet Boys wailed.

He took my face in his hands and kissed me in a way I'd never been kissed before. His tongue down my throat, nearly gagging me, the scruff of his slight mustache and chin hairs chafing. When he finished, I felt as if I'd been devoured. Even though I was shocked, I had to admit it felt great. With Maisie, we always kissed respectably, usually without tongues, like an elderly couple on a park bench.

"You liked it," he said, under his breath.

He lay down on his bed and patted the spot next to him. I still was trying to catch my breath, as if he'd sucked the life out of me. Part of me imagined I'd join him on his bed, but I was scared for what might happen next. Scared to go any further because of Maisie, and because I'd never really gone further than a kiss with anyone else.

A trickle of blood leaked from my nose.

"You're bleeding," he said, as if I was a nuisance.

"Oh crap." I caught the blood before it hit his carpet.

"You get a lot of nosebleeds, don't you?" he asked, one of his eyebrows questioning.

I wiped my nose with the back of my sleeve. "Uh, I should go."

He yawned. "All right."

"I'll see you at work tomorrow," I said.

As I left, I could see him reaching for the pipe

again, already bored of me and moving on. I darted down the stairs and out of his house. I gulped the air, trying to get my heartbeat back to normal, but it was no use. My heart thumped so fast, I thought it'd explode from my chest.

I licked my lips that could still taste Doug, a grape flavor from the Bubble Tape gum he'd been chewing.

I wondered if every time I'd taste grape for the rest of my life, I'd think of Doug. And how he'd stolen my breath that afternoon.

Chapter Twenty-One

My high from the kiss didn't last long because as I stepped outside onto Doug's front lawn, I sensed someone creeping up from behind. I chalked it up to being paranoid from the pot we smoked, but before I could even turn around something jumped on my back. I swiveled around to throw it off, but whoever it was held on tight. I started freaking out, flinging my limbs as I was brought down to the grass. I heard the person mumbling, "Eliminate the threat. Eliminate the threat." Oh, hell no. I wasn't gonna be eliminated in a timeline before I was born. So, I kicked back as my attacker flew off of me.

The sun had set, the block poorly lit. It was difficult to see who it was, but I instinctually knew. The spikey-haired woman. Sure enough, from the light of the moon, her spikes sparkled. She was holding the gun. I scurried up on my feet and put my hands in the air. My luck, the first time I really smoked pot and I get mauled.

"I'll shoot you," she said, spittle flying from her mouth.

"I-I believe you."

"Good." She swiveled her head, likely to check if anyone was around. The block empty. Typical Frontier, Iowa. Where nothing happened until something really bad happened. "Take me to your base."

"My wha…?"

"Your base!" More spittle spurted from her lips. "Where you're rebuilding the time machine."

"You wanna go back to the present?"

A deadly smile trickled up her cheek. "I have other ideas where I want to go."

"What does that mean?"

"Shut up. If you take me there…" She seemed to be figuring out the next steps. "I won't kill you. You can stay in this era for all I care."

I was trying to stall while I figured out the next steps too. Even though my weed-addled brain made that difficult. "Why did you jump with us?"

She pounded her chest. "I've worked for Omni for decades and what have I gotten in return? Nothing. He's never taken me seriously."

"Who? Horatio? Mr. Thoorai?"

She nodded with a trace of respect. "I see you've met his earlier iteration."

"Yours too."

"Yeah, what's she like?"

"I'm not a fan."

She thrust the gun closer to me. "This is how it's going to work. You will take me to your base, and only once I've jumped, will you and everyone you care about be safe."

"Okay, okay, my bike is here."

"You'll sit in my lap and pedal with the gun to your back."

I walked slowly to the bike. "Why did you stay so long at Omni if you hated it so much?"

"I didn't hate—I said I was never respected. Scoot and Horatio were dead set in their war against each other and my ideas were discarded. But it wasn't always like that. Before Scoot came along, Horatio and I were a team. Us versus the world. We'd speak of all the times we longed to visit, to make the world a better place. Events we could prevent from happening in the past. Knowledge we could accumulate from the future. The world was teetering precipitously, but we could realign its values, its tenets. And then Scoot showed up. A brilliant mind—I couldn't compare, even with all my years as a scientist. Horatio started seeing how much money he could make off of the time machine, not using it just to forward society, but to forward himself. Scoot too, they were both greedy in those early days at Nimo. Before Horatio took the company back. But it was already too late. The rot had started to seep in. We no longer spoke of the magnificence we could achieve, only dollar signs. And I was regulated to being his lowly assistant."

My bike leaned up against the tree. I considered making a run for it and chancing that she wouldn't shoot. But her eyes were so crazed, and she foamed at the mouth like a dog. I wasn't dealing with a rational mind here.

"But if Scoot didn't exist," she said, coming alive. "If I went into the deeper past and destroyed him when he was born…"

"Kill baby Hitler."

"What? Well, yes. In a sense. Your grandfather is baby Hitler."

I clenched my fists. "If you kill my grandfather, then I won't exist."

She made a mopey face. "Ah, that's the rub, isn't it?"

"Rub this." I lunged at Irma, knocking her to the ground. The gun went off. A few birds escaped to the sky. We rolled around as she tried to line up a shot again. I grabbed her head with the intent to…I didn't know what I intended to do; I just was working on instinct. I smashed her head into the ground once, enough to hear a loud thunk. Looking down, her head bashed into a sharp rock. An alarming amount of blood leaked from the back of her head. She made a strange sound, a mix of a gasp and a cry. I leaped off of her, shaking. Her body began to twitch. She found my eyes, looking as if she wasn't ready for whatever was about to occur. The blood flowed from her head like a river.

"Uh…." I said, because I was still high.

I grabbed the gun, which had fallen from her hands, and stuck it into my waistband.

As I was about to make a dash for my bike, Doug stepped out of his house with a garbage bag thrown over his shoulder.

The garbage bag dropped to the floor. His mouth wide open.

"Alex, what the f—"

"I can explain," I said, no clue how I might start.

―――――

"This feral woman attacked me," I said, pointing at her as if it was obvious. "Like a hill person, she came from the hills."

"Iowa doesn't have hills," Doug said. "Is that a gun in your waistband?"

I went to cover it up better, but the gun fell out to the ground. I scooped it up.

"Hey," Doug said, throwing up his hands. "This isn't some feral woman."

"No, okay…" I bit my lip, figuring out how much to say. Working at Omni, he knew the possibility of a time machine. It wouldn't be too much of a leap. "What if I told you I'm from the future?"

"What?!"

"I'm Miles," I said, relieved because it was getting hard to remember to call myself Alex. "My brother Simon created a time machine in 2024. We came back in time to help my Mom, Patty—that's Scoot's daughter. He hits her, all because he gets pushed out of the company by Mr. Thoorai, so we're trying to prevent that."

Doug slapped his forehead. "A time machine? Gnarly. Mr. Nimo and Mr. Thoorai were coming close, at least from our testing but a component was always missing. The H-caliber lunar function—"

"Right. Completely, the H-caliber. It's the worst."

Doug grinned. "All very impressive." His eyes clicked over to the body. "But there is a dead woman on my lawn."

"She tried to shoot me. And we were wrestling—she hit her head on a rock."

"I can see that. Lucky it's dark, although this block is always deader than dead. Sorry, poor choice of words."

"What do we do?"

"*We*?" Doug asked. "How am I roped into this?"

"Uh, she's on your lawn."

Doug nodded. "Okay, I dig. Good thing you're a good kisser, Alex…Miles."

"So, you'll help?"

"We'll throw her in the car and take her to the trash heap."

Doug got her head and I got her legs as we carried her into the garage. We propped her against the wall. A trail of blood leaked from the lawn.

"That's a lot of blood," I said.

"I'll put on the sprinklers," Doug said, and manually turned them on.

We opened his trunk and heaved her among tennis rackets and a spare tire. She looked peaceful all curled up inside.

"Shit," Doug said. "Is that Irma? Like, a super old Irma?"

"It's the Irma of 2024."

"You really didn't like her, did you?"

I put my hand on my hip. "I didn't do this on purpose."

He closed the trunk. "Sure, Miles."

We drove to the garbage heap. I remembered going when I was kid. I'd thrown out my stuffed animal Penguiy (he was a penguin), and my dad took me to the dump to find it. Not a successful mission, but I appreciated his idea. It reminded me to spend more time with teenage Kip if I had the chance. Mom was the target, but he'd be a key to making her better.

Doug turned on the radio to break the awkward silence, Lit's "My Own Worst Enemy."

Doug crooned: "It's no surprise to me I am my own worst enemy."

Was I being my own worst enemy? First, killing Irma by accident and then spilling everything to Doug. I watched him driving. Was he someone I could really trust? Besides the make-out session and that he loved Creed, I didn't really know anything about him.

"You can trust me, Miles," he said, as if he could read my mind.

"I wasn't thinking I couldn't."

"You'd be crazy not to. At this point I'm an accessory to the crime."

"In 1999, there would be no surveillance cameras. No one would have seen me, unless you have a nosy neighbor."

He shook his head. "The light was out in front of my place. They couldn't have seen anything in the dark."

"Thank you for helping me," I said, twiddling my thumbs. "You're like, really cool."

His metal braces gleamed. "I know that." He reached over and tousled my hair. "You're pretty cool, too. Jumping through time like it's nothing."

"It's not nothing."

He snapped his fingers. "Your nosebleeds. I should've been suspicious."

We reached the trash heap and took the body out of the trunk. She looked frail, but was heavy. I started to cry.

"Hey," Doug said. "No, don't do that."

"She's dead." Her mouth stayed open in shock. "All because of me."

"She tried to kill you."

"But if I just got the gun from her…"

"She wanted to kill your grandfather so you wouldn't be born. She deserved this."

We tossed her down a heaping pile. Watched her roll to the bottom.

"What happens when they find her?" I asked.

"This gets cleared once a week. So, it'll be a while. And then, we're each other's alibi. Also, this version of her doesn't exist in 1999. They'll think she's some…" He smirked at me. "Feral woman from the hills."

I managed to laugh a little. "I couldn't think of anything else."

"Yeah, I got that."

We headed back in his car. I needed a ride to the underground lab and was so tired, I didn't have the strength to do anything but be driven. He fiddled with the radio as we headed into the dark. He sang The Fly's "Got You Where I Want You."

Got you where I want to.

I felt Doug take my hand. Mine was so sweaty I was embarrassed. My heart still thumped like mad. These past few hours had been a whirlwind.

"Breathe," he said.

"What?"

I was having trouble breathing.

"When we're in shock, we forget to breathe."

I gulped a big breath and felt a little better.

"Thanks," I said. "For everything."

"Don't think of it." He slowed the car down. "This where you're supposed to be?"

"Yeah," I said. I could see the trapdoor from the car window. "Thanks."

"You already said thanks."

"I-I mean it."

"If I can help you in any way. At Nimo…? What's the next step?"

My head ached. I winced in pain. "This put a wrench in it for sure. I'll have to tell Simon…"

"What if you didn't tell him?" Doug asked. "This could be our secret."

"I don't know."

He pulled my hand up to his lips and kissed it. "I like you, Miles."

"I like you too, Doug." I thought of Maisie. "But I have a…"

"Girlfriend. Yeah, I know. But she didn't help you today."

"No, she didn't."

He let go of my hand and kissed me on the lips again. On the radio, the Verve Pipe's "Freshman" played. *For the life of me…* I kissed him some more. *I could not remember.* I lost all sense of time. *What made us think we were wise?* He wouldn't let me go, like we were fused together. *We were only freshmen.*

We kissed until the song ended, then I broke away and opened the door without looking at him again, as if I was ashamed. Either of cheating on Maisie, or what I'd done that day. What I could never return from.

"She's alive," he said, when I was outside, through the car window.

"Huh?"

"She's still alive." He lowered his voice. "Irma. In 1999. So, you didn't really kill anyone."

I shoved my hands in my pockets.

"Chin up," he said. "Stud."

I cracked a smile as he gunned the gas and drove away. The faint sound of Semisonic's "Closing Time" hanging in the air.

You don't have to go home but you can't stay here.

I climbed down the trapdoor.

Chapter Twenty-Two

As I scrambled down the ladder, I debated how much I was gonna tell everyone. While no one would be happy with me killing Irma from the present (even though it was an accident!) at least we didn't have to worry about her sneaking up with the gun. Which, by the way, I now had in my possession. So, a bit of a mixed bag all around...

"Who are you talking to, Miles?" Simon said. He sat at the table by the entrance with Mr. Congley. A million papers scattered between them.

"No one...myself. What are you both doing?"

Mr. Congley tried to organize the papers. "We're still missing a part. I sent out an order for it, but can't seem to find the bill of sales."

Simon gave me a look. "We're dealing with a Mr. Congley in this era who's a little bit green."

"Hey," Congley snapped. "I'm sitting right here. And I've put you up in this underground lab, so you can at least be thankful."

Simon stood and walked over to me. "What's wrong?"

"What's…what?"

He crossed his arms. "I can tell when something's wrong with you, Miles. You talk to yourself."

"I do not." I tried to move past him. "Quiet," I said, under my breath.

He snapped his fingers. "There! You're doing it right now."

"Balls," I said, punching my thigh.

Simon grabbed my arm and swung me around. "Okay, have out with it. What's happened?"

I took a big breath. "Okay, remember that spikey-haired woman?"

Simon pinched the bridge of his nose. "Of course, I remember."

"She might be dead."

"Might be?" Congley asked.

"Oh no," I said. "She's a hundred percent dead. She tried to murder me because she came to the past to get a time machine and go back even farther to kill baby Hitler, I mean, our grandfather."

"She what?" Congley asked.

"The spikey-haired woman is also Irma, the lady who works at Nimo."

Simon nodded. "I should've realized. Now that you say it, I can see the similarities."

I attempted to smile. "So, it was good that I killed her, right?"

Simon fixed his glasses on his nose. "It's never good that you killed someone."

I stamped my foot. "But you said before that we might have to…take out Mr. Thoorai. How is this any different?"

Simon started pacing. "Hold on, let me think. Okay, you killed the Irma of 2024, which means Irma in 1999 is still alive."

"Duh."

"The big question: Will she be there in 2024 when we return?"

Mr. Congley threw up his hands. "If you can return."

"What does he mean by that?" I asked.

"Meaning we still need this one part," Simon said.

My voice got really small. "And if you can't get it?"

"Then get used to 1999."

I gulped.

"How did you dispose of the body?" Simon asked. "Irma."

"The garbage dump."

"All by yourself?"

I ran through scenarios of what to say. Simon was already pissed about the murder and wouldn't be too pleased to hear Doug was an accomplice. Better he would never know.

"Yeah, totally all by myself."

"No one saw you?"

"The street was empty."

"How did you get the body to the dump?"

"…On my bike."

"You pedaled all the way to the dump with a dead body?"

"It was really close."

Simon gazed at me closer, looking for telltale signs I was lying. I gave him nothing.

"All right," he said. "Hopefully this doesn't come back to bite us."

I whipped out the gun. "And I have this now."

"Chekov's gun," Congley said quietly and went back to sorting papers.

Simon marched over. "Give me that." He took the gun.

"Why do you have a gun?" I heard, and we all swiveled around.

Maisie stood at the foot of the ladder. She'd been crying, I could tell. Her face reddened.

"Are you okay?" I asked, as I attempted to go over to her.

"No," she screamed. "I saw my mom."

———

All of us were stunned.

"You saw your mom?" I asked. "Are you sure?"

"Yes, I'm sure." She pushed past me, got a Kleenex, and blew her nose.

"Your mom who's been traveling through time?" I asked.

"No." She blew her nose. "The young version of my mom. I recognized her."

Simon ran over and grabbed her by the shoulders. "Did she see you?"

"No," Maisie said, and wrenched away. "I don't think so. I dunno. I mean, this mom doesn't know who I am. And why do you have a gun?"

Congley cleared his throat. "Miles killed the spikey-haired woman."

"It was an accident!"

"You killed her?" Maisie asked, overwhelmed by all the news. She rubbed her forehead. "What does this mean?"

"It's okay," Simon said. "It doesn't change anything. What was your mom doing?"

Maisie managed to smile trough the tears. "She was riding a bike. Her dress flowing. She looked so graceful. She was happy, I could tell. She must have been eighteen or nineteen, like in college."

"Do you remember where she went to college?" I asked.

Maisie shook her head. "Probably in the Midwest, I dunno. I wanted to say something. I mean, I know I couldn't, but I wanted to. Just to hear her voice."

"Did you see where she went?" Simon asked.

Maisie nibbled on her lip. "She was biking toward Nimo."

"Can you tell us what she looked like?" Simon asked. "Talia, right? That's her name?"

Maisie started crying again. "She has long brown hair. Ultra-long, like down to her waist, and big, beautiful blue eyes. When she smiles, she shows all of her teeth."

"We'll look out for her," Simon said.

Maisie went over and pushed him. "And then what? What does that mean?"

"Maisie, she is a variable we can't predict," Simon said. "We can't know how to act until it happens."

"I want to meet her," Maisie said. "At least for a second."

Simon fiddled with the glasses on his nose, a sure sign he was rattled. "All right, I'll figure it out. You have my word. For now, let's get some rest. It's been a hectic day all around. Tomorrow we're gonna go to the physics club early, since it's a Friday and only a half day at Jeremiah Boonton. We need to check up on Mom…" He coughed. "I mean, Patty…and Kip."

"Right, the mission," Maisie said, as if she was defeated. "Always the mission."

Maisie rubbed her eyes and lurched off toward the bathroom. I went after her, but Simon stopped me. There wasn't much free space in the lab where she could go, even though she probably needed to be alone.

Simon's eyes told me to grant her that, so I did.

I listened, for once.

Chapter Twenty-Three

At the after-school physics club the next day, me, Simon and Maisie sat at a table with Kip and pretended to do the calculations that Mr. Congley gave us. Well, Simon did them in about three and a half seconds, but that wasn't a surprise. Maisie seemed glummer than usual. She was doodling a picture of a woman getting sucked into a vortex. A girl who looked like her was reaching out to save the woman, but was too far away. I definitely interpreted that this was her mom.

"You okay?" I asked, hesitant to hear her response.

She stabbed the paper, tearing it to pieces. The Britneys glanced over and giggled.

"None of it matters," she said, under her breath.

"What do you mean?"

She gestured around us. "This isn't reality. Not ours."

"It is because we're in it."

Simon glared for us to be quiet, as Kip raised his eyebrow.

"We got high before class," I told Kip, and he nodded.

"I'm sorry if I've been preoccupied," I murmured to Maisie.

And kissed someone else, I wanted to say, but imagined she'd go nuclear.

Maisie shook her head. "This isn't about you, Miles." My eyes bugged. "Sorry, Alex." She lowered her voice even more. "I want your mission to be successful, really, but *I* have a mission now. Don't you see?"

"I understand," I said, feeling horrible. "I've been selfish. What can I do to help?"

"Let me come with you to Nimo," she said. "So I can talk to my mom."

"What will you say?"

"I don't know. I—have a few ideas. I just want to get to know her. Who she really is."

"It's an internship, Maisie. I don't get to say who can come."

She pinched my leg under the table, twisting the skin hard. "That's not a good enough answer. I can blow up your whole spot."

"You wouldn't."

We were snapping at each other. Kip leaned over.

"Everything all right between you two?" Kip asked.

Maisie gave a moony smile. "Just a lover's quarrel."

Kip raised his palms, like, *keep me out of it.*

The Britneys passed over their BFF book. The question this time, written in glittered marker was: *Which one of us Drives You Crazy?*

When I looked over, they each blew a bubble with their gum.

Maisie grabbed the book and scribbled, *Simon, let*

me come to Nimo tomorrow or I'll stand up right now and tell everyone who we are.

She shoved the BFF book at him. He read with a perturbed frown. Maisie began to stand, but Simon gave a cool nod and she sat down.

She took the BFF book back, crossed out what she wrote, and scribbled instead: *He is MINE, you clones. So back off! Or I'll hit you baby one more time.*

She tossed the book at them. I didn't have a chance to see their reactions since Patty walked inside. She floated over to the table like a zombie, like the mom I knew from the present time. When she sat next to me, I understood. She'd taken pills, the ones she'd become addicted to that kept her stable but robbed her soul.

Me and Simon locked eyes, sad for this demise. If we were already too late...

"Patty?" I asked.

It took what felt like years to turn toward me. "Yes?" she said.

My voice wavered. "What's wrong?"

"Hmmm?"

"You seem..."

"I can think now," she said. "I can shut out the noise."

A few years ago, when Mom starting getting worse, I'd try to get her out her funk. I'd do a dance, make a joke—sometimes she would surface from wherever she went and laugh or join me dancing, as if she became free from the spell she was under. But soon, nothing I did seemed to help. Once she went under, she was fully submerged.

"What noise?"

She scratched her arm. But the itch wouldn't go

away. She scratched harder and harder, digging through the sweater until she poked a hole.

She chewed on a piece of hair. "I don't want to talk about it here."

"Things at home?" I asked, and she gave a grave nod.

There was no way I'd let her go back to her house after school, at least not until nighttime once her parents would be asleep. There was also no way she could come down to the lab. I was sitting between her and Kip, so I turned to him.

"Hey," I said, even though he had his nose firmly planted in a book.

One of his eyebrows raised.

"I'm worried about...Patty," I said, trying to be as quiet as possible.

"How do you mean?" Kip asked, still without a clue. I wasn't surprised that my young dad was just as self-absorbed as he was in the present time.

"Look at her." I nodded over as we watched her gnaw on a piece of hair. "Her home life is a disaster."

He still had his nose in a physics book, able to multitask. "Yes, it was very uncomfortable being around her parents."

"It's abusive. She's been hit."

His other eyebrow raised. "Really?"

"Yes, her dad hits her mom and then her mom hurts her. It's a fucked-up cycle."

We looked over as Patty smiled into space.

"She looks happy right now."

I slapped my forehead. "She's self-medicating. Don't you see that?"

I wanted to yell at him for years of frustration. How he enabled Mom. Would give her all her pills.

Keep her numb. Because the alternative in his eyes was way worse.

He snorted. "Didn't you say you were high right now?"

"It's different," I said, especially because I wasn't high right now, unless if I'd remained stoned from the night before.

I had a flash of wrestling Irma and her head knocking against the rock. A pool of blood leaking from the wound as the life left her eyes. I shook it away. I had to focus on Mom.

"She needs supportive people around her," I said. "She shouldn't be taking pills."

He shrugged his shoulders.

"She cares about you. She told me."

Now he took his nose out of the book. "Really?"

This was a bold-faced lie, but I figured I'd run with it. They wind up together anyway, so what would be the harm?

"She wants to get to know you better. And since it's not safe at her house, what if we went to yours after?"

"Oh," he said. "You all wanna come over?"

"Yeah, we can be your wingman. Get you guys together. You like her, don't you?"

His face turned red. "No, I mean, I don't know."

"You do. I can tell from the way you look at her. You guys would make a great couple."

"We would?" His voice hit a high octave.

"Let us help you." I put my hand on his shoulder. "Because I think it would help Patty too."

"I do…I do want to help her."

"The kind of pills she's taking, it's no good. We gotta get her to stop doing that. Take her mind off of what's going on at home."

"It's just—my house is nothing to brag about. It's small. Just me and my mom. She gave me the bedroom and sleeps in the living room. After my dad died, well, we didn't have enough money to keep our old house."

"I'm sorry." I was tearing up. I killed me to hear how hard Dad had it.

"She works a few jobs—my mom. So, she won't be home. It's messy but…"

"We don't care. Maisie won't care. It's a safe space. Your mom loves you a lot and you love her too."

"Of course, she's sacrificed a lot for me."

"It'll be good for Patty to be around that. We can make it a regular thing."

Kip glanced at his physics book. "I usually just study when I get home."

"Do you ever *not* study? You gotta live a little."

"Yeah," he said, and then repeated as if he really needed it to sink in. "I did just get an A on my last test."

"Good." I turned to the rest of the table. "Kip invited us all to his house after."

Patty let the piece of hair fall out of her mouth. Her smile wide.

"That's sounds wonderful," she said, as if she was sailing on a cloud.

Chapter Twenty-Four

Kip's house—I was getting a lot better at not calling him dad—was small but had a homey feel. My grandma Denise, who I'd only seen in pictures, put up paintings of ducks along the walls. A fireplace mantle held photos of Kip as a little kid with a gap tooth smile. Denise had rosy cheeks, built like a bear. In every picture she was hugging him. I could feel the love through the photos. There was one of Kip as a baby in a man's arms I assumed was my grandfather. Dad never spoke of him, since he was a toddler when he died. If he spoke of his mom, it was always quick. I could tell he never got over her death.

We went upstairs to a hallway with a bathroom on one end and Kip's room at the other. Inside on the wall, he had a giant poster of Einstein making a goofy face.

"Einstein," Simon said. "You a fan?"

"He's only the greatest genius of all time," Kip said, practically foaming at the mouth.

The two of them started discussing Einstein's greatest

hits. I'd let them have this bonding session. In the present time, they weren't close since Simon was always so busy. I also felt like Simon never really respected Dad. Simon would never settle for being a math teacher at a community college, with one invention failing after the other. He knew deep down Dad had the potential, but wasn't utilizing it properly. Mom probably had a lot to do with that, since she sucked up his energy. Another thing we could hopefully fix if we got to go back.

Maisie went over to Kip's stereo. She popped out a Mozart CD and held it up.

"Got anything current?"

"There's one song I like," Kip said, and rooted through his desk finding a New Radicals CD. "You Get What You Give."

On the cover, the singer wore a bucket hat with Vans shoes.

Maisie played the song, which I had to admit was catchy as hell. She started dancing in the middle of the room.

I went over to Patty, who sat on the window sill staring out at the street.

"Hey," I said, sitting next to her.

Once again, she took a long time to turn toward me. "Hey, Alex."

"Are you okay? Seriously."

She leaned close, whispering. "I'm trying."

"I'm asking this as a friend. Okay? I think it's important you have friends you can tell things to."

"I think so too."

"What did you take?"

I looked in her eyes, but they gave me nothing.

"Take?"

"Patty, you're fucking high," I said, and then reined it in. I was speaking from frustration. All the years she remained numb when I wanted a mom.

"But it doesn't hurt anymore."

"What?"

She unrolled her sleeve, showing her bruise.

"Is this a new one?" I asked.

"She was drunk last night, really drunk. She broke a bottle."

"Grandma Ill?" I said and slapped my hand over my mouth. But Patty didn't notice.

"No, my mom," she said. "Dad didn't come home last night. He never doesn't come home."

"He must've been working late."

She shook her head. "He doesn't want to be home. Around her. Or me. We get in the way."

"Of what?"

She managed to laugh. "Of his dreams. Time…"

"You don't think he really built a time machine? You know that's impossible."

"Nothing is impossible. It just hasn't been done yet."

What if I told her? Who I was. Who'd she become. Would that convince her to stop?

But I couldn't. It was too dangerous.

"The pills are no good for you," I said. "Don't take them."

Her smile turned venomous. "You're not my mother."

"No, I don't hit you."

She gasped. "Fuck you."

I'd never seen a side to her like this. "Patty—"

"No, who are you to tell me what to do? I ate a

bunch of pills yesterday and now I don't want to cry myself to sleep, so how can that be bad?"

My eyes welled up. "Because you'll get addicted."

"It's still better if it erases the pain."

I grabbed her by the shoulders. "You'll become a zombie, Patty. Do you understand that?"

"Let go of me."

I was shaking her now. "No, I'll lose you."

"What are you talking about?"

We were yelling over the song.

> *But when the night is falling*
> *You cannot find the light*
> *You feel your dreams are dying*
> *Hold tight.*

Maisie stopped dancing. I was still shaking Patty, trying to get her to wake up. Simon and Kip came over.

"Hey, stop," Simon said, pulling me off.

"She's not listening." I was fully crying now. "She's hurting herself. It'll be too late. It's already too late."

Kip was giving Simon a strange look. Under his breath, Simon said, "Our mom."

Patty became inconsolable. She writhed around. When I tried to grab her again, she slapped me across the face. The sting throbbing.

Maisie ran over and was hugging her, trying to calm her down.

Kip put his hand on my shoulder. "Your mom is like this?"

I wiped my eyes. Glancing at Simon, he gave a tiny nod to continue. "Worse," I said. "She's been coping with pills for years." I pushed out a heavy breath. "She was abused, it's the same thing. She's a zombie, and she's never there for my brother or me. Now she's in a home, like a place for people like her. She bit a nurse. All we want to do is for her to get better."

I hugged Simon, leaning on his shoulder.

"Our dad enables her," Simon said, speaking to Kip like he's always wanted to talk to Dad in the present time. "He does it because he loves her so much, but it's no good. She's in a facility now, but he took too long to get her into one. It may be too late."

Kip spoke quietly. "How does he enable her?"

"Just plies her with pills," Simon continued. "I think in his mind, he's convinced they balance her out and without them she'd be suicidal. It's only been a few days since she's been in the facility, so we don't know if she's gotten any better. It's why we've been spending time away...from Elgin, from home. We're scared to see what it'll be like when we get back."

This was too much for me. Seeing my mom wail with Maisie attempting to get her to stop screaming. I couldn't be around it.

"I'm sorry," I said. "I gotta go."

I was out the door before anyone could stop me. I ran down the stairs, barely able to see because of the tears blurring my vision. When I got downstairs, my Grandma Denise had stepped inside and was taking off her coat.

"Oh sweetie," she said. "Why are you crying?"

I couldn't even begin to explain, so I rushed into her arms. She was startled at first, but then gave me a bear hug. She smelled like apple cider. Her hug so warm I never wanted to let go.

So, I didn't. Time owed me that.
This moment I could make last for an eternity.
Even death not keeping us apart.

Chapter Twenty-Five

Hard to wrap my mind around hugging a dead grandmother I was never supposed to meet. It made me think about how time really worked. I looked at a map of my life, born in 2010 and living through 2024 with a tiny gap for a week when I went back, and now in 1999 for as long as we'd be here. This 1999 that existed now changed forever. And would still keep changing until we figured out how to go home. I became overwhelmed. Even back home, I didn't have someone who could give me a hug and make me feel better. Sure, things had gotten better between my dad and me, but he wasn't really the comforting type. Not for more than a minute or so. Simon was a robot. And mom—she once was comforting. I remembered being very little and her waking me up early in the morning to watch the sunrise. This was as she started to turn. She said the sun was like her lifeline, keeping her tethered, as if she knew she was about to go dark. She'd hug me as the sun kissed my face. It was the last time I ever felt safe.

Until now. From the little I heard about Grandma Denise from Dad, she was a martyr. She worked two, and sometimes three jobs after her husband passed. She was a bus driver and then a waitress at night. Hugging her, she still hadn't taken off her apron, done with a shift and probably getting ready for her next one.

She gave me a last squeeze. "Oh, hon, what's wrong? Are you Kip's friend?"

Stunned, I worked my mouth to finally speak. "We're in physics club together."

She waved at the air. "Nothing I understand."

When she laughed, her whole body jiggled. She had big cheeks like she was hoarding food and a button nose.

"How'd you like some pie?" she asked and shook the bag she was holding. "I brought it home from the diner. Apple, it's fresh."

I was still having a hard time speaking.

"I can add a dollop of Breyers ice cream."

"Okay."

We went into her kitchen, where she sat me at the corner table with doily placemats and made us plates. She put a heaping of ice cream on the pie and popped it in the microwave until it melted into the crust. I wolfed mine down. Instinctively, like a grandma would, she spoiled me by cutting another slice.

"So, what's got you down, love?" She smiled, her cheeks pink. "Trouble at school?"

I shook my head.

"Your family?"

I nodded.

"My mom's not well," I said.

She put her hand on her heart. "Oh sweetie, I'm so sorry."

"They put her in a place, like a home for crazy people."

"Tut tut, they're not crazy." She wagged her finger. "They just have a harder time at things than us. She doesn't mean to be like that."

"I know, but she also took pills that made her that way."

Denise cleared her plate in the sink. "I remember my father; he was a gambler. When I was little, he did quite well. Would come home with presents all the time: a toy horse, a beautiful doll. He was my hero. But then he started losing and he came home sad, so sad. It wasn't the father I recognized. He didn't want to be like that, but sometimes we forget that our parents are people too."

"No, I know...my mom had a tough childhood, her parents... It wasn't good. It's how she copes."

"Ah." She scooted to the refrigerator. "Can I interest you in some lemonade?"

"Sure."

She danced over and poured it for me in a glass with duck decals. It was pure sugar and so good.

"My father got better," she said. "Had many years until his end that were lovely, peaceful. He quit gambling. Oh, it was worse before it was better, that's usually how it goes. But then it did get better. And he was sorry. He apologized to me when I was a young adult in my twenties. It took him that long, but he got there. And I forgave him. Because what's the point of holding onto hate? That's what makes us sick."

I cringed, knowing she would get sick and die from breast cancer. We would have this conversation, this pie, and that would be all. I wanted to hold on to it for as long as I possibly could.

"So, here's my advice…"

She looked at me to say my name.

"Miles," I said, not even thinking to lie.

She touched my chin. "Miles. Young Miles, if you forgive your mother now for all of her shortcomings, you won't allow that anger to make you sick. Because she will get better. I can sense that. I can sense things. Even if it's a little in the future, it will happen."

My mouth got very dry. "How can you sense things?"

Her eyes sparkled. "Just that your story won't end badly. A hunch."

She handed me a handkerchief of hers emblazoned with ducks and I blew my nose.

"Kip is lucky to have a mother like you."

She rested her hands on her stomach. "You're lucky to have your mother too."

I felt the sun washing over my face, from when Mom and I would watch it rise.

I once asked if it rose only for us.

"Yes," my mom had said. "Because we've been good and deserve it."

Then she gave me an Eskimo kiss.

"I hate to cut this short," Grandma Denise said, standing and taking my plate. "But I have to get to work. Bus driving in the morning where I wear flats, come home and change to kitten heels for my diner shift, then pumps for the night haul. But you stay as long you need to, Miles. Is Kip upstairs?"

"Yeah, with the rest of the physics club."

She clapped. "Oh, I love to see he's made some

friends. My Kip has a hard time letting people in. Always with a nose in a book."

I grinned. "Yeah, I'd agree with that."

"But he's a good kid. He takes care of his mom. He likes to take care of others. It's in his blood."

She was right. After she would die, he'd devote his life to taking care of Mom.

"But I want him to live more," she said. "Outside of a textbook. The whole world isn't physics. So, I hope to see you back here, Miles. It's been lovely sharing pie with you. And I hope you're feeling better."

I stood. "I am. Can I get a hug for the road? You give really great ones."

"Oh, sweetness, sure."

She dwarfed me in a hug as I took in her cider scent for one last time.

Committing it to memory even after I'd let go.

Chapter Twenty-Six

It was barely morning when Simon woke me. I was having the dream of me and Mom watching the sunrise during better times. He shook me, causing it to shatter. "Let's go," he said, pulling me from my mattress and tossing the sheet to the side. Over in the corner, Maisie stirred but her eyes didn't open. Simon put his finger over his mouth. I followed, still tearing sleep from my eyes.

We got on our bikes as we pedaled into the dawn. We were quiet at first until we'd fully awoken.

"I promised Maisie she could go to Nimo too," I said. "To see her mom."

"Negative," Simon replied, as if there would be no argument.

"Hey," I called out, since he was pedaling faster than me. "You're not the boss of everything. She's gonna be pissed that we left without her."

"So, let her be pissed." He slowed until we were biking next to one another. "Mom got worse after you left."

My stomach did cartwheels. "How do you mean?"

Simon's tone got serious. "She had more pills with her. She took them when we weren't looking and barricaded herself in the bathroom. Luckily, Kip's mother…"

"You mean Grandma Denise."

Simon pinched the bridge of his nose, not wanting to be interrupted. "Yes, Miles, I am aware of that. Luckily, she'd already left for work when it happened."

"She's pretty great," I said as Simon raised his eyebrows. "Grandma Denise. She gave me a big hug. I was crying."

"What did you tell her?"

"Nothing. I just said my mom was having issues and it was tough living at home. We never really got the chance to have grandparents. Good ones."

"Anyway," he said, changing the subject. Typical Simon. Hard to tell if he ever had emotions. He'd get rid of them as soon as they popped up if they could affect the mission. "I wanted to get to Nimo early today to do some spying. We're almost reaching the point in Scoot's journals when he signs over the company. There's no use staying here if we fail at that. And Mom might already be too far gone now."

"Maybe there's other ways to save Mom?"

"Don't be naïve, Miles. Optimism won't save her."

For the first time since we jumped, I had the nagging feeling we wouldn't be successful. Even if we wound up returning home.

"Any word on the part you're waiting for?" I asked, hopeful for one ounce of good news.

"Congley's working on it today," he said as we reached Nimo and parked our bikes.

We scanned the IDs they made for us and went

inside. No one had come to work yet, the offices hollow and echoing. Except for voices at the end of the hall. Simon gestured for me to follow and we crept down a metal hallway, trying not to make a peep. At the end, the voices rose in volume. Scoot and Mr. Thoorai.

"Do you really think that's best?" This was Scoot.

"It is our only option," Mr. Thoorai replied.

"But a foreign adversary?"

"You equate adversary with foreign, but that isn't a given."

"It's not a certainty they won't be an adversary," Scoot said. "Look at history. We're only a decade out of a forty-year Cold War."

I caught Simon's eye, both of us in fright. We mouthed, "Russia."

"This will help ingratiate ourselves with them," Mr. Thoorai said. "Once they see the machine."

"Do you mean the United States, or just Nimo?" Scoot asked.

Mr. Thoorai didn't respond.

"Horatio," Scoot said. It was the first we heard Scoot use Mr. Thoorai's actual name."

Horatio's voice rose. "You do not have your eye on the prize."

"And this prize, what is it?"

"Power. Money. What else do we strive for?"

"To better society?" Scoot asked, as if he was afraid.

"I've seen a peek into the future, and it is not so grand. In two years, America will be attacked unlike we've ever seen. Planes will be used as weapons."

"He's talking about 9/11," I whispered to Simon.

"Thank you, Miles. I'm aware of this," Simon said.

"Which means Horatio has been to the future," I said.

Simon shook his head. "He probably did what I did at the beginning of my experiments, travel for a minute or two. There's no way they have the capabilities yet for more than that."

The two men started shouting at one another through the metal door.

"I have someone on the inside," Horatio said.

"Who?" Scoot asked. "In Russia?"

"A consigliore, a go-between. Putin wants this."

"Putin? The Prime Minister?"

"He will be president very soon. He will pay us a fortune."

"To hand the time machine over?"

"When it's finished, yes. And we'll build another one, a better one with the money we'll get."

"This isn't what I've signed up for, Horatio."

We heard the sound of a *thwack*. Horatio had likely hit Scoot.

"You are a horrible alcoholic, Scoot. You are hanging by a thread."

"All you are is money, Horatio," Scoot said. "You don't have the mind for time."

"Then why have I been able to see glimpses of the future, while you are stuck here?"

"Because you've gone before I said it was ready."

Horatio thundered: "*I* say when we're ready."

Scoot roared back. "The science says when it's ready."

"The consigliore is here in town, a young woman," Horatio said. "She's been the go-between back and forth to Russia for the better part of the year. Smoothing relations."

"I refuse to let my invention be sold to a foreign—"

"This is where you are wrong, Scoot, because like I've told you, I've seen glimpses of the future. And in that beautiful future, you are too weak of a man to run this company and have given it over to me."

"Never."

"Never is a strong word, my friend."

"We are no longer friends," Scoot sneered.

"We never were. We used each other. And now, your use has ended."

We heard them rustling. As the door opened, we ran down the hallway and rounded the corner.

Their footsteps fired against the metal floor.

When they turned the corner, Horatio gave a look of surprise at us while Scoot seemed too forlorn to glance up at all.

"Young men," Horatio said, chewing on the words. "Got here earlier than usual."

"That's who gets the worm," Simon said, not showing any sweat.

"Precisely," Horatio said and turned to Scoot. "You can learn a thing from this generation." He reached into Scoot's lab coat pocket and pulled out a small bottle of bourbon. "If you were lucid enough this morning to realize."

Horatio smirked and continued along, whistling.

"I have my eye on you, boys," he said. "Consider me impressed."

He disappeared down another hallway.

Scoot stared at his hand that shook. He grabbed it with his other hand to settle.

"Get to work," he said, waving us away.

As he was about to leave, I stopped him. He looked at me with glassy eyes, already accepting his defeat.

"Don't let him win," I said, as Scoot narrowed his eyebrows.

"Alex…" Simon said, pulling at my sleeve.

"No, there's no more time," I said. "We're already into October. You wanted us to be your eyes and ears here."

Scoot shook his head. "It doesn't matter anymore."

"You're weak," I said.

Scoot shook his head in disbelief. "Who do you think you are…?"

"I'm your ghost of Christmas Future," I said.

He stared at his hand again that quivered like mad. "I must be drunk."

"You must be, but that doesn't mean you can't listen. He's gonna try to get you to sign over the company."

His voice was shaky. "Who…?"

"Horatio!" I yelled, and quieted myself.

"How do you know his actual name?"

"Because we're your eyes and ears here," I said. "He's going to trick you. Don't let him."

"The devil wears many disguises."

"I know that," I said, pointing at Scoot. "He's standing right in front of me."

"Alex…" Simon said again, yanking at me harder.

"No, he needs to hear this." I thrust my finger in his face. "You are the devil. The devil always invades those who are too weak to keep him away. You hurt those you love."

His chin began to shake, tears forming in his foggy eyes. "I don't mean to."

"Doesn't make it right. Patty is…she's our friend. And you've hurt her."

"No, never, I've never hit—"

"But you've hit Lillian, who has then hit her."

"No, she wouldn't…"

He reached out to get me to understand, but I swatted his hand away.

"The best thing you could do is vanish before you infect them anymore."

"You are a…you are a child. You know nothing."

"You are an adult who knows even less," I said, reining myself in so I wouldn't spit on him.

The front door opened and Doug walked inside.

"What's going on here?" Doug asked as Scoot gathered himself together.

"Nothing," Scoot said, sucking back tears. "Everyone get to work."

He marched off as Doug turned to us. "I always found him to be a weird dude."

"You're not the only one," Simon said, letting me go.

"We have something to ask you," I said to Doug.

"We do?" Simon questioned.

"Yes, is there anywhere we can go in private?" I asked.

"Where we first met." Doug smiled. "The bathroom."

Chapter Twenty-Seven

On our way to the bathroom, I realized Simon didn't know I'd told Doug about the time machine. Surely, Doug would bring it up in private and I'd be screwed. My forehead began to sweat, palms clammy. Simon noticed. There was no way to put anything past him.

"What's wrong?" Simon asked.

"Uh…" I spied Irma at the end of the long hall. "It's Irma, she'll be suspicious that the three of us are going into the bathroom together."

Simon frowned as he clocked Irma and headed toward her. "I'll keep her preoccupied."

With Simon taken care of, I pulled Doug into the bathroom.

"Whoa," Doug said as we entered. "Somebody's getting rough."

He pinned me against the wall and attempted to give me a kiss.

"We don't have time for that," I said, pushing him away.

I went over to the sink and turned on the faucets.

"Just in case they're listening. I overheard Mr. Thoorai talking with Scoot. He wants to sell the time machine to Russia."

Doug cackled. "Russia? C'mon."

"He says there's a woman working for them. I… forget the word he used, consigliore?"

"Oh yeah, she just started here. She's a little bit older." He winked. "College girl. She was flirting with me."

I rolled my eyes. "I doubt that."

"Does that make you jealous?" he asked.

I shoved him. "What do you know about her?"

"She's a Russian studies major, spent a semester in Moscow. That's how she was hired."

"What's her name?"

"Talia."

I tried not to show my shock about hearing Maisie's mom was the go-between Omni and Putin. I shouldn't be that surprised, since her father Smith was rotting in prison for being a stone-cold murderer. Her mom would stay working at the company long enough to be sent back in time years later only to disappear. But she didn't seem to be a killer like Maisie's father, not from the way Maisie described her.

I went to leave and tell Simon, but Doug grabbed my arm.

"I gotta go," I said.

He trickled his hand down my arm. "Stay a little."

We heard a loud knock at the door. Doug let go.

"This company you work for," I said, under my breath. "It's evil."

He pulled me toward him and gave a quick kiss. "What do they say about keeping your enemies close?"

"It's time to start work," we heard shouted from outside. Likely Irma.

"Let's hang at my place again," Doug said, cupping my chin.

"O...kay," I said, but I knew I shouldn't. It wasn't right to cheat on Maisie like this. I needed to tell her the truth about what happened at Doug's the last time and about her mother too.

Doug went to the sink while I grabbed a paper towel, dried off, and tossed it in the garbage. When I exited, Irma was standing at the door with a scowl.

She showed me her watch. "You are wasting time."

"We got here early."

She turned on her heel and proceeded to walk down the hall. "Time is still wasting."

I watched her ahead of me, knowing I'd be responsible for her end.

When we reached the end of the hall, she was about to leave but I stopped her.

"Why do you work here?" I asked.

She scowled even more. "What kind of question is that?"

"Don't you have a passion?"

Caught off guard, she made a squawking sound. "My passion is working for Mr. Thoorai."

"When you were a little girl, didn't you have a dream?"

"Where is this coming from?"

"We all have dreams," I said. "Didn't you want to be something more than this?"

She huffed, clearly annoyed with this conversation.

"I wanted to be a detective," I said. "Like my idol Sherlock Holmes. I wanted to help solve mysteries."

She pawed at her purple hair that was already molding into spikes. "Baked goods."

"What was that?"

"I...always had a talent for baking. Desserts. Maybe own a dessert shop."

"You should do it."

"That's nonsense. This is what I do."

"What if what you do gets you killed?"

The air filled thick with a heavy tension. I was going too far. She looked deep within me, scouring my soul. When she blinked, I could tell she had gotten spooked. She turned around to run away. Her high heels clacking down the hallway. Glancing over her shoulder in fright.

What was she scared of?

Had she seen the truth and her inevitable death?

And had I gone too far by making her aware?

Chapter Twenty-Eight

After a morning of pretending to do work, I told Simon I couldn't focus. The ones and zeros were making my vision blurry. Simon, on the other hand, had already finished a stack and was waiting for a refill.

"You really gave it to Scoot," he said, chewing on a red pen.

"He deserved it."

"No argument there. Maybe tough love like that convinces him not to sign the company over."

"What else can we do?" I asked, feeling like I needed to go back to the lab to tell Maisie about her mom.

"You seem on edge," Simon said.

"Okay." I leaned in closer to him. "Maisie's mom is the go-between. The consigli—whatever it's called with Russia."

Simon eyed the camera in the corner of the ceiling.

I drummed against the table out of nervousness. "I need to tell her." I already stood up, not backing down.

"You're leaving?"

"I can't sit here drawing circles on these fucking papers."

"What will telling her accomplish? She'll freak out. Kill the messenger, i.e., you."

I was at the door. "I'll take that risk—"

"Miles," he said, but I'd already left. I ran down the hall.

At the end of the hallway, Scoot leaned against the wall in deep thought.

"I...have a stomachache," I said. "I need to go."

He barely registered a response.

"Did you hear me?"

His bloodshot eyes drifted over. "Do you really think I'm the devil? I set out to do good."

I just wanted out of there. "Things got warped."

"How can I absolve myself?"

"Don't let Mr. Thoorai take this company from you. And if you can't be a positive role model for your daughter, it's better if you just leave, vanish."

Like a child, he looked at me for answers. "Where can I go?"

"Far enough away, so you can't hurt your family anymore."

He crumpled like I'd punched him in the stomach. I didn't have time to deal with my dumb grandfather's fragile ego. I swiped my ID through the scanner and left. Got on my bike outside and pedaled fast as I could back to the underground lab.

When I arrived, Maisie was in the spare room painting. I watched her for a moment. She'd recreated our entire journey through art. Starting with the tunnel we jumped through to get to the past. Another of the underground lab. The picture of her mother being sucked into a black hole. The work was beautiful, haunting. Clearly, she'd found the inspiration she thought she lost in the present.

"You left without me this morning?" she said flatly.

"I know, we wanted to get to Nimo early—"

"I'm not a thought to you, Miles."

"That's not true—"

She spun around, splattering me with paint. "You never wanted me to come to the past." She ran her fingers through her hair, coating it in reds and blues. "You told yourself you did, so you could pretend to be a good boyfriend."

"I am a…" I stopped myself because I was far from being good. Images of kissing Doug flashed.

She smirked. "Can't even finish the sentence, can you?"

"I have something to tell you," I said, gaining the courage.

She shrugged as if she couldn't care less.

"You're right, I haven't been a good boyfriend. I kissed someone else."

She crossed her arms. "So did I."

"Who? That art guy with the JNCO jeans?"

"What if I did? But no, it was this girl…"

"A girl?"

"His friend. Kate. She's like me, artsy, loves Jeff Koons. Like, we had this great conversation over coffee about his talent."

"I don't know who that is."

"Exactly, Miles, we don't have a lot in common. And like, we're fifteen. I don't think I'm ready for a serious relationship. We don't even know if we're gonna get to go back home."

I gazed at my shoes to avoid looking at her. "We will."

"Why? Because has anything worked out during this trip so far? It's been a disaster. Look, it's okay you kissed someone else. I'm letting you be free."

I kicked at the floor. "I don't want that."

She raised her voice. "Well, I do. Kissing Kate, like, it was better than you. Softer. Different."

"Now you're just being mean."

"Fine, if you need to think that—"

"Your mom is at Nimo."

She rushed toward me, practically knocking me over. "Wait, you saw her?"

"No, but I know what she does there. She's working for Russia."

"What?"

"She's the go-between for Putin. So Russia can buy Omni's time machine and then Horatio can build an even better one with the money they get once they boot my grandfather."

Maisie massaged her forehead. "I don't believe that."

"It's the truth!"

She spun around and clocked me in the face. "No! You're just saying all of this because I rejected you."

"I wouldn't do that."

"I don't know *what* you are capable of doing anymore, Miles. I don't know who you are. So, leave me alone and go keep kissing whoever's dirty lips you were. Because you'll never kiss mine again."

"Maisie…" I went to grab her, but she wrestled out of my arms and started hitting me.

"Get out." She took a deep breath and roared. "GET OUT!"

She pushed me hard, flinging me out of the room and slammed the door. I fell on my butt. I got to my feet and pounded on the door, but she wouldn't open it. I could hear her crying, feeling horrible. But I deserved it. I had treated her poorly since we arrived, took our relationship for granted.

After pounding on the door to no avail, I gave up. Maybe she was right that we were too young for a serious relationship. Maybe she only wanted to be with girls after all, and I couldn't compare with Kate.

I found myself jealous of this mystery girl. Whoever she was. I needed out of that lab, far away from Maisie as possible. Doug had invited me over, and honestly, that afternoon in his room had been the best part of this whole stupid journey. Everything else seemed to be a failure.

There was nothing else I could do for the mission, so I climbed out of the lab, hopped on my bike, and rode to Doug's.

Part of me wanted to kiss him again.

To feel like I was getting even with Maisie.

Chapter Twenty-Nine

Doug opened the door gobbling from a bag of Munchos. He was barefoot in baggy jeans with an oversized Creed shirt. What can I say? The guy liked Creed. On his shirt, a clay man erupted from the earth.

"Come in," he said, swiveling around. An old dog slobbered over.

"This is Igor," he said.

I gave Igor a hug, needing some love.

Igor seemed indifferent to my embrace.

Up in his bedroom, Doug flopped on the bed and played air guitar to Creed's "With Arms Wide Open." It smelled of shwaggy weed and incense at war with one another.

I pushed aside a pile of clothes to sit.

"I broke up with my girlfriend," I said, sniffing back a tear. I didn't think it'd be possible to get back together with Maisie after the things we said. She didn't care, that was clear. So, neither would I.

Doug whistled. "I bet you could use…" He held up a pipe filled with pot.

"No, I'm good."

The last—and first time—I smoked pot, I wound up killing someone. I didn't want to risk it.

"C'mon, drown out your sorrows."

Doug took a drag and blew smoke at me that wet my saliva buds.

"You're better off," he said, indicating for me to take a hit while it was still burning. I shrugged and took a puff, started hacking.

"How can you do your job if you're getting high all the time?" I asked once I stopped my coughing fit.

"That's precisely how I *can* do it well. You need a vice in life."

I took another drag. "Nothing goes right in my life. Everything I came here to do has gotten fucked…"

"Yeah, I want to hear more about your time machine." He indicated to pass over the pipe and inhaled. "Mr. Thoorai has traveled back, but only for a few minutes. That's all it let him do. What's the secret?"

"Fuck if I know. I'm science stupid."

"How is that possible? You got an internship—"

"Simon got the internship. He just talked his way into convincing them to give me one too."

Doug narrowed his eyes. "So, you don't know how the time machine works?"

"Can we not talk about time? It's all I've been focusing on since I got here and I'm sick of it."

Doug beckoned me to join him on the bed. I lay next to him as "With Arms Wide Open" continued.

Doug put his hand on my cheek. "You've sacrificed a lot to be here."

"Yeah, everything. My whole life in 2024, even though it was kinda boring. My detective agency wasn't going anywhere and it seemed every day me and my friend Kevin would go to school where we were invisible. I thought going back in time, saving my mom—I dunno, doing something that had meaning… You can't run away from your problems, I guess, even twenty-five years into the past."

Doug blew a smoke O. "Yeah, I totally get that, man."

"And we might not get the part we need to go back. Maybe we should've never played with time. At least for the second time. Ugh, I'm high—"

He kissed me, tasting of potato chips. His tongue flicked around, aggressive, the opposite of Maisie who kissed so sweetly. I already missed her.

Doug's hand moved down my shirt toward my pants.

"What're you doing?" I asked.

Doug grinned. "What I can tell you want." He started singing, "I just want to say hello again."

His fingers played with my jeans button. I leaped out of bed.

"What is it?" he asked.

"I…uh…have to take a whiz."

"Down the hall on your left."

Out in the hallway, I could breathe again. I wasn't ready to go further with Doug. Despite being high, my failures were messing with me. Killing Irma, not helping Mom get off pills, destroying my relationship with Maisie. I went to go splash water on my face, but saw a closed room across the hall. I expected it to be Doug's brother's room, the jock. When I opened the door, it was empty. Not an ounce of furniture. Odd. I left it and walked down the hallway to a room at the end that should be Doug's parents' bedroom. The church-looking folks. But when I opened it, the same thing, an empty room like no one lived there.

I shut the door that made a loud sound and went into the bathroom. A toothbrush and toothpaste rested on the sink. I turned the faucet on. Through the wall, the Creed song ended, and I heard Doug shuffling around. He put on Eve 6's "Inside Out."

"Wanna put my tender heart in the blender," he sang through the walls. I could relate. My heart was beating like mad. I put my ear against the wall. Eve 6 still blared, but I thought I picked up Doug's voice too. Maybe on the phone. I cupped my hand over my ear to listen better. In between the thumps from my heart, I heard Doug speaking…

In Russian.

I slipped, cracking my head against the floor and making a thud.

Eve 6 stopped.

I bit my lip, listening to any sounds through the wall. Doug stopped speaking in Russian. And at all.

He put on another CD. Rob Zombie's "Super-beast," the beats thudding through the floor.

The music cranked up louder until it was shaking the house.

I heard a knock on the door. "Everything all right in there?"

I gulped, my Adam's apple bobbing up and down. "Yeah." It sounded like I was going through puberty again.

The door opened and Doug stood there, one hand behind his back.

"Hey now," he said. "I'm the one that you wanted. Hey now, I'm the superbeast."

"I fell," I said, my ears hurting from the volume.

He leaned down. "You were snooping. I could hear you closing doors."

"Why are those rooms empty? Where are your parents' and your brother's rooms?"

He cracked his neck. "I don't have parents or a brother."

"No?"

"*Nyet*, Miles." He shook his finger back and forth. "Doug is a creation." He had a thick Russian accent now. "What an American boy should be. Listen to Creed music, ha ha. They are *mycop*. That means garbage in Russian. We spit on them in the motherland."

"What do you want?" I asked, my teeth chattering.

He revealed a gun from behind his back.

"Your time machine, Miles. For if the motherland can get a better one for free, why should we pay Nimo?"

"We're still missing a part. Remember?"

He shoved the gun in my face. "I want to see what you have so far."

"It's my brother Simon, he knows about everything. I told you, I'm science stupid."

He yanked me up by my collar. "Then we go to your brother. Where is he now?"

"At Nimo still. I left, but he stayed to work."

He pushed me ahead of him. "Then we go to Nimo. *Dvitgat'sya*."

The hallway shook from the music as he led me with the gun at my back.

"Was any of it real?" I asked over my shoulder.

I felt his lips graze my ear. "I was told to do anything and everything by my government to get the time machine. So no, none of it was real. You were foolish, and I could tell you liked me, so I used that."

Down the stairs, we passed Igor the dog, who gave a sad fart. I should've picked up on the fact that his dog had a Russian name. My detective skills had certainly gone down the toilet.

Outside, Doug shoved his keys into my hand as we got to his car.

"You drive," he said.

"I don't have a license! I can't drive a car."

He cocked the gun. "You will figure it out."

"I will figure it out," I repeated.

I got in the driver's side and turned on the ignition. Backstreet Boys "Larger Than Life" came on. He sat next to me, the gun poking my ribs.

"This is more my style of music," he said, singing every lyric with perfection like he was frickin' AJ in the band. "You had found my secret before."

"To each their own," I said, trying not to show the disdain on my face. "I should've realized from the frosted tips."

"Floor it," he screamed in my ear.

I slammed on the gas as we careened out of his driveway and "Larger Than Life" pumped from the windows.

Chapter Thirty

With the gun pressed into my back, Doug led me into Nimo. Since it was early, barely anyone was there. I figured Simon had already left to go to the physics club, or back to the lab, which was why I brought Doug here. At least I'd have time to figure out what to do next.

"Faster," he said, pressing me harder with the gun.

"Sorry, Doug," I said, thinking of ways to stall. "Or whatever your real name is."

"It's Alexi."

I slapped my forehead. "That's so funny. I pretended to be Alex, and you *are* the Russian version of Alex."

"Shut up."

Our footsteps echoed as we reached the hallway. The room they put us in was at the end. I took a deep breath, opening up the door and praying Simon had left.

But there he was. Finishing the last sheet of papers from a tall stack.

Alexi shoved me inside and shut the door with a slam.

"So, we have a problem," I said, as Simon registered the problem by sliding his glasses up his nose.

"Yes, big problem," Alexi said.

Simon coolly placed his finished paper on top of the stack. "I take it you're after the time machine?"

Alexi seemed shocked. "Yeah, I'm after the time machine."

Simon did not show an inch of fear. "And from your accent, I'm guessing you are a Russian spy. Likely from Southern Russia."

"What, how did you know that?"

Simon stood, bored with the conversation. "I could tell from the dialect. The Central Federal District."

Alexi took the gun off me and pointed it at Simon. "Sit the fuck down."

Simon shrugged. "You don't have to be so crude."

Alexi shook his head. "No, stand up. We're getting out of here. You know what I want."

Simon gave a cocky grin. "What is it again?"

Alexi stamped his foot. "The time machine."

Simon tapped his chin. "Oh right, right. And why do you want this?"

"You…" Alexi began before shooting the gun at the wall. We all jumped. "I am serious. You see that?"

Simon raised his hands. "Yes, yes, I do. Very serious."

Alexi blew out his cheeks. "My government told me to do whatever it takes to get it. Spying at Nimo. Or kissing your brother."

"I still believe you liked it," I said.

Alexi swatted at me with the gun. I imagined my face turning black and blue.

"Everything's a joke to you, isn't it?" Alexi said. "You've never waited in a line for bread like I have. You Americans have it so easy, life is not pain."

I gritted my teeth. "I've experienced pain in this life. My mom—"

Alexi threw up his hands. "Yeah, you said she's vacant or something. Big deal. You didn't watch her be executed. Like I did. My whole family. My father. My brother. Shot one by one down the line."

"And this is the government you work for now?" I asked.

"I don't have a choice."

The door flung open and Scoot barreled inside. He was a withered version of the man we met, the last few days destroying his psyche. He managed to have lost weight; his pants barely held up by a belt.

"What's going on here?" he asked.

He cocked the gun and raised his hands.

"Shut the door," Alexi ordered. "Stand by the two boys."

"Your accent…" Scoot said. "Are you…?"

"Russian, yes," he said. "Working for the other team like you Americans foolishly say. And what the hell is this place, Iowa? Cornfields and cornfields. Who can eat that much corn? Corn is hard to digest."

My stomach rumbled from thinking about eating corn. "Tell me about it."

"Shut up," Alexi thundered. "All of you. Why can't you just shut up?"

"We're shut," I said, waving my hands. "All the way shut."

"What do you want?" Scoot asked, getting serious.

Alexi gave a wide smile, his braces beaming in the

fluorescent light. "Miles, why don't you tell him who you are?"

Scoot ran his fingers through the little left of his hair. "Miles? I thought you were Alex?"

"Uh…"

Scoot turned to Simon. "And you were Matthew?"

"Negative," Simon said.

"They are your grandchildren," Alexi said. "From the future."

Scoot's mouth dropped. He began shaking, then got himself together.

"The time machine?" he said, stuttering.

Alexi laughed. "What a genius you are, Scoot. Really figured it out."

"But why did you…?" He looked to me for answers, our previous conversations making more sense. "You're Patty's children? She becomes a mom? I'm a grandfather?"

Alexi rubbed his eye with his free hand out of frustration. "Yes, that is how it usually works."

"What did you come to the past for?" Scoot asked, turning to Simon since he likely realized I was the dumb idiot when it came to any sciencey explanations.

"You lose Nimo," Simon said.

"So, you came to the past to save Nimo for me… why? What happens?"

"Mom turns into a shell," I yelled, catching everyone off guard. "A shell of who she used to be. She used to be the best mom, but her abuse catches up with her and she takes pills to numb. I told you that you hurt Lillian, who then hurts Mom. We want to stop that cycle!"

Scoot was silent.

"Nothing to say?" I kept yelling. "You're a horrible person. You're greedy. And she suffers."

Scoot glanced up, as if he'd been through a war that scarred him. "Patty's an addict?"

"She's in a fucking institution in 2024," I said. "And it's all because of you."

"All right, enough," Alexi said. "You're taking me to the time machine to hand it over and anyone who gets in the way, I put a bullet in their brain."

But no one was listening to him.

Scoot stared at his trembling hands. "Lillian, she... doesn't understand the importance of what I do. That's why I hit—"

"Stop making excuses, you asshole," I said.

"You can't speak to me that way," Scoot said. "I'm your grandfather."

"Maybe by blood," I said. "But not in my heart. We never meet you. You die from alcohol poisoning after you sign Nimo over during a blackout. My mom and your wife don't even go to your funeral."

"Ahhh," he said, clutching his chest. He let out a cry. "Ah, ah, ah." He began hitting himself in the chest.

"Stop that," Alexi said.

"Let him abuse himself, he deserves it," I said.

Scoot's cries became louder.

"Shut the fuck up," Alexi yelled. He ran over to try and get Scoot to stop hitting himself.

"No, let him hurt himself," I said, shoving Alexi's shoulder.

Alexi trained the gun on me. "I am getting *very* tired of you, Miles."

"Nah, you love it when I push you."

Scoot screamed, causing us all to cover our ears.

Alexi lost focus for a second, and I went for the gun. Alexi and I rolled around on the floor as I tried to grab it from him. He gnashed his teeth, his braces snapping at my nose. I pushed him off and scrambled to my feet.

"You are irrelevant, Miles," Alexi said, getting to his feet too. "Simon is the brains and who I need for the time machine."

He pointed the gun at me, flirting with the trigger.

Scoot kept moaning. "I'm dead, I'm dead, I'm dead."

Alexi spit. "Yes, you're goddamn dead in the future. What's so hard to understand?"

"I never got to be your grandfather," Scoot said, and we locked eyes. I saw his pain, his sadness. Who he became that left him miserable. "I'm sorry," he mouthed.

I didn't know how to respond. Too worried about the gun trained on me.

"Don't shoot him," Simon said. "I'll take you to the time machine."

Alexi smirked. "Yes, you will. But it's too late for your brother. Say goodbye."

He squeezed the trigger as the world shifted to slow motion.

"Nooooooo," I heard Scoot yell as he dove in front of me, taking the bullet. It clipped him in the chest, blood spurting from his lips. He crashed to the floor.

"Dammit," Alexi said.

Out of the corner of my eye, I saw Simon running into Alexi and knocking him to the ground. The gun flew from Alexi's hands. I went to go pick it up when Scoot grabbed my arm.

"I'm sorry," Scoot said, blood spilling at an

alarming rate from his mouth. "Tell Patty I'm…sorry too."

I gulped a breath. "Okay. You took a bullet for me."

"Don't ever say your grandpa didn't do anything for you." He winced, holding his chest. "Get the gun."

I dove for the gun as Simon and Alexi fought. I pointed it at them. "Stop," I yelled.

Alexi looked like he wanted to murder me. Again. He spit on the ground. "He's dead."

When I looked over, Scoot's eyes were wide open, his mouth slack.

I burst into tears, overwhelmed by it all.

"Hey," Simon said, rushing over and taking the gun. "Let's deal with him first."

"Okay," I said, but as I handed the gun over, Alexi flew to the door, opened it, and burst into the hallway.

We made a dash to catch up with him, but by the time we left the room, he already disappeared. The sound of his footsteps getting fainter until they stopped completely.

We looked back into the room where Scoot's blood was leaking outside.

Simon shut the door. "Let's get out of here."

I caught my breath. "All right, where? Where do we go?"

Simon rubbed his forehead. "Congley's still waiting on that part, so no point in going to the lab. The time machine is safe, but Mom…"

"What? What about mom?"

Simon swallowed. "I'm afraid he's gonna go after her to get us back."

My heart froze. "Okay, okay, let's go."

We ran outside and spied a bike parked, so we got

on it. Simon pedaling like mad as we flew to Mom's place, hoping Alexi wouldn't beat us there.

Had we come to the past to save Mom, only putting her in worse danger?

I shuddered at the thought.

Chapter Thirty-One

We pounded on Mom's door, glancing over our shoulders to make sure Alexi wouldn't sneak up from behind. Mom opened it, confused, and I'd forgotten that she was still mad. She was about to slam the door, but I blocked it with my foot.

"What are you doing here?" she asked, as Simon and I flew inside.

"It's not safe," I said.

Grandma Ill walked in from the kitchen, wobbly on her feet and likely already smashed.

"What's the ruckus?" she asked, hiccupping.

"It's your father," I said to Mom. "He…"

I didn't even know how to begin to explain. I just wanted to get her out of the house as fast as possible before Alexi might show. I looked over at Simon, who was just as lost but at least more logical.

"He's missing," Simon said.

Grandma Ill nearly fell over. "What…?"

Mom twisted her sleeves, her anxiety evident. "I don't understand."

"Mr. Thoorai wants your dad out of the company," I continued. "And will do anything to get rid of him."

"So, he vanished," Simon said. "The last we saw him he was…drinking."

We eyed Grandma Ill, who was having difficulty standing. She let out a howl.

Mom covered her face. "Mom…"

"No," Grandma Ill yelled and marched over to Mom. "You did this."

Under her breath, Mom whispered, "You're drunk too."

"I am completely lucid," Grandma Ill said. "You drove your father away!"

"That's not true," I said. "Scoot couldn't deal with being forced out of his company, so he fled."

Grandma Ill pulled at her hair. "He would never leave us."

Mom was crying now. "He hits you."

"You be quiet, child. You don't understand the sacrifices one makes in a marriage."

"I know abuse shouldn't be one of them."

Grandma Ill slapped Mom across the face so hard it brought Mom to her knees. She quivered on the floor. Grandma Ill leaped down to attack her more, landing blow after blow until I jumped between them.

"No," I thundered at Grandma Ill. "You will not hit her anymore." I was grabbing Grandma Ill by her arms, ready to hurt her too.

"Stop," Simon said, trying to pull me back.

But I only saw red. Ready to destroy Grandma Ill for all the pain she caused Mom.

"You do *not* get to hurt her." I let go of her as she collapsed to the floor, shaking.

"C'mon," I said, taking Mom's hand and leading her out of the house with Simon behind me.

Grandma Ill still wailed. "Then don't ever come back, you worthless worthless child."

I covered Mom's ears so she wouldn't have to hear. She was quaking in my arms. Simon hopped on one bike, and I got on Mom's that lay beside it—pink with a basket holding a CD Discman. I lifted Mom up so she sat behind me and put her hands around my waist.

"I know where I can take you," I said, whispering in her ear.

She nodded through the tears as we pedaled away.

Night had fallen, the streets dark and empty.

We rode in silence until we reached Dad's house.

The safest place I could imagine for Mom to stay.

Chapter Thirty-Two

Dad was flummoxed to see us when we arrived. Mom in tears, Simon and me trying to catch our breath. I didn't think Alexi knew who he was, since I only mentioned my mom, so we were likely safe. Dad had a textbook in hand and headphones around his neck that played classical music.

"Come in, come in," he said. "Are you okay, Patty?"

She shook her head and seemed so fragile that he put his arm around her shoulders to lead her inside. It was sweet to see them this way—what their marriage was probably like before Mom started to disintegrate.

We sat on the couch and told him everything that happened. Well, nothing about the time machine, of course, only what happened with Scoot, Grandma Ill and Mom.

"It's not safe for her to live there anymore," I said, as Mom put her face in her hands.

"Do you have any relatives you could stay with?" Dad asked, but she shook her head.

"Both my parents are only children," she said.

"Can she stay here tonight?" I asked.

"Yeah, of course. I mean, I'll ask my mom when she gets home, but it should be okay. We turned the attic into a spare room. It's really small, like the ceiling is five feet, the whole house is small. But there's a bed and a window."

"Thank you, Kip."

"Do you need anything?" he asked her. "Are you hurt?"

"A little sore."

"Hold on." He leaped up. I'd never seen my dad with so much energy. When he came back, he had two bags of frozen peas. "Here, for your bruises."

Mom held one over her arm.

"Your cheek," he said, because it was starting to turn a different color. "I can…" He rested the other bag of peas against her face.

The door opened and I jumped out of fear. Nervous it could be Alexi, but it was just Grandma Denise wearing her waitress apron. When she saw us, she put her hand to her mouth.

"Oh, what happened?" she asked, rushing over.

"Mom, this is Patty," Kip said. "My…friend. And my other friends, Alex and Matthew."

Luckily, too much was going on for Denise to realize that I'd been called Alex when I told her my name was Miles.

She went over and inspected Mom. "Did you fall?"

"No," Mom said, as if she was embarrassed. "My parents…" She broke down in tears.

"Oh, sweetie," Denise said, and gave Mom a hug like she'd done to me. Mom rested on her giant bosom. She stroked Mom's hair as she eyed all of us. "Why don't you give us girls a moment? Kip, take them up to your room."

We followed Dad upstairs. In his bedroom, we paced around, not knowing to do with ourselves.

"I didn't realize how bad it was for her," Dad said.

I picked up a Slinky just to give my hands something to do. "Worse than you can imagine."

"My mom's the type to let her stay forever," he said.

Simon and I looked at one another. Maybe that would be the key to saving Mom? Away from Grandma Ill, she wouldn't have the need to turn to pills.

"You care about Patty, don't you?" I asked.

His cheeks turned red. "I always had a crush on her, but didn't think she noticed me. Since no one really does."

"You two have that in common," I said. "But she notices you, trust me."

Dad's eyes bugged. "Oh yeah?"

"Yeah, so take care of her."

"I will," he said.

"You're a good guy," I said, slapping him on the back. "I don't say that enough."

Simon slapped Dad on the back too. "Neither do I. But you really are."

Dad couldn't hide his smile. "Thank you. That means a lot. Like I said, I don't really have friends." He nodded to his textbook, as if it was the culprit for his social status.

I gave him a hug. "You do now."

He was hesitant at first, but then managed to hug back.

The door opened and Denise entered. She gave us

a rosy smile. "So, I have to change and get to my next shift, but Patty is going to stay with us for a while. Okay, Kip?"

"Told ya," he said to us.

Denise put her hand on her hip. "What did you tell them?"

"Only that I had a great mom," he said.

"Well…" She chuckled. "That girl could use a good home for a bit. Away from her mother at least. And if the woman has an issue, she could bring it up with me. Sweet Patty is grabbing her CD thing from outside. Give her space when she comes up."

She winked and went to close the door, but I slipped outside. My heart firing into my chest.

Denise rested her hands on her stomach. "Hello, Miles. What can I do for you?"

"Uh, thank you for taking Patty. When I saw her mom hitting her—"

Denise held up her hand. "You did the right thing bringing her here."

"Also, uhh…have you ever gotten a mammogram?"

Denise tilted her head to the side. "Now why would you go asking that?"

"My…my aunt, she…they caught something recently, but it's okay. They caught it before it spread. So, she told me to warn any women who maybe hadn't been checked out. That it's worth doing."

She cupped my chin. "What a curious child you are."

My eyes watered. "Please, tell me you'll do it. Please."

She shuddered, as if I had goosed her. Letting go of my chin, she nodded.

"Okay then. I will. Happy?"

I sighed the longest sigh ever. "Very."

"Now I gotta scoot before I'm late for work. You take care now."

"You too Grand—Ms. Hardy."

She titled her head again out of confusion, but then just waved me off and continued down the hall to her room.

Satisfied, I went downstairs and found Mom outside by her bike. She had put her headphones on, listening to music I could hear blaring.

"Can I join you?" I asked.

We sat against the edge of the house.

"What are you listening to?" I asked.

She took off her headphones and flipped them over so she could place one against her right ear and the other against my left one. We listened to "Freak of the Week" by Marvelous 3.

"Sometimes I feel like the freak of the week," she said, eating her tears.

"Hey, you are not responsible for your parents being assholes."

She laughed at that. "It's not funny. I don't know why I'm laughing."

"Because it's better than crying."

She leaned her head on my shoulder, the music pumping between us.

"It'll be better for you to stay here," I said. "Kip's mom is a really good person. And he cares about you."

"My mom will throw a fit when she finds out."

"Let her. She deserves to lose you."

She let the words sink in before speaking again. "I can't thank you enough."

"You don't have to thank me. Thank you. For being amazing."

She took her head off my shoulder. "How is it that you always manage to say the right things?"

"When I was younger, my own mom taught me well."

Simon stepped out. "I'm afraid we should be going," he said.

I stood up and handed Mom back her CD Discman.

"You keep it," she said. "For whenever you feel like the freak of the week too."

"We're headed to Elgin," I said, my voice getting chopped up from the tears coming on. "Probably no more physics club. It's time for us to get back."

"Oh, I'll miss you guys," she said. "I hope you won't be a stranger."

Like a punch in my gut, I managed to say, "I hope you won't be a stranger too."

We hugged and I didn't want to let go, but eventually Mom did and shuffled back into the house. Simon squeezed my shoulder.

"You okay?" he asked.

"Not in the least."

"We saved her," he said, showing the tiniest hint of a tear that I'd never seen before. "Now it's time to go home and make sure it worked."

"What about Alexi?"

"Once we're gone, there's nothing he can do since we'll take the time machine back with us."

"What about the part you're missing?"

"We just have to have hope that it finally arrived."

"I didn't think a science man ever relied on hope."

"The universe is a mysterious place," he said,

taking in a deep breath of air as a change washed over his face. We had been through a lot, and we'd come out of this journey different. Even Simon.

He got on the bike and I climbed on too, hugging my brother from behind. Normally, he would've swatted any affection away, but he had no choice.

I was able to hug him all the way to the underground lab.

Chapter Thirty-Three

We climbed down to the lab to hear good news from Congley that the missing part, the H-caliber thingamabob, had finally arrived. He was screwing it in the glove that appeared to flash and glow once it was inserted. We explained our mom was safe now and there was nothing left to do here but go back.

"No!" Maisie said, overhearing and storming out of the room with her paintings. "I never got to see *my* mom."

"Maisie, she's working for the bad guys," I said.

"You got to save your mom, and I'm supposed to, what, just go home without even trying to save mine?" She seemed like she wanted to spit on me. "How is that fair?"

"It's not, but think logical."

"Oh, fuck off, Miles."

Simon blocked her as she tried to leave. "Maisie, what's your plan?"

"I don't know, go down to Nimo and try to get her

to not work for them anymore. So she'd never go missing."

"It's not that simple. She's essentially a Russian spy."

Maisie went to hit him, but he blocked her. "Out of my way, Simon!"

"You can't go down to Nimo because there's a dead body there."

Congley stopped tinkering with the time machine glove. A perturbed look crossing his face. "What did you do?"

"Our grandfather is dead," Simon said. "The other Russian spy there killed him. Scoot jumped in front of a bullet that was meant for Miles."

"It was pretty heroic," I said. "Even though he's an asshole."

"He would have died soon anyway, so it shouldn't disrupt our regular timeline," Simon said. "But I wouldn't recommend you going down to those offices now, Maisie, and we don't have time to wait for you to come back."

Maisie punched the wall. "It's just not fair."

"None of it is fair," Simon said. "And this doesn't mean we couldn't do a future jump to save your mom too, but not in 1999, we'd have to go back to before she began work as a Russian consigliore."

Maisie broke down in tears. "I just miss her, and my dad is in prison so I have no one. My grandparents, they resent me, I can see it in their eyes. I remind them of the daughter they lost. And everyone at school hates me and my artwork. Like, I have nothing in 2024 to return to."

"Hey," I said. "You have us."

"Right, you hate me too, Miles. And Simon, you've disliked me since we got here."

"I don't hate you," I said. "We had a fight. And we fought hard because we love each other."

She sniffed up a booger. "You love me?"

"Of course I do." I went over and put my arm around her. "You mean everything to me. I'm upset you kissed someone else, but I could never hate you."

She gave a fake punch to my gut. "I could never hate you too."

"We have to go," I said. "The guy I kissed, who I thought was named Doug, is a Russian spy too. He tried to shoot me. He would have killed me if not for my grandfather taking the bullet. He wants this time machine glove and he'll stop at nothing to get it."

"But we're safe in this underground lab," Maisie said. "How long does it take to boot up the glove?"

"Around an hour," Congley said.

I was quiet.

"Miles, why didn't you answer her when she asked if we were safe?" Simon said.

We heard rustling above us. The sound of feet scampering, voices shouting that reverberated down.

"What are you not telling us, Miles?" Simon said, always able to ferret out if I was lying.

"Doug—I mean Alexi drove me back here," I said, unable to look him in the eye. "After we got high and I killed Irma by accident, I was shocked."

Simon's face burned red. "So, you took him here?"

"He drove me! I wasn't thinking straight. I just killed someone. By accident!"

Simon's eye twitched now. "Miles, why didn't you say something before?"

"I knew you be mad."

"I am *beyond* mad. I'm in a whole new world of anger you can't even imagine."

"I think I can."

The voices above us got louder. They seemed to be circling directly over the trapdoor. But they didn't know the code. Fuck, I realized. The code was Nimo. How could we be so careless?

We heard gunshots. It didn't even matter for them to try the passcode. The trapdoor unlocking from the bullets. Our assailants rushed down the ladder.

First Alexi, with a gun trained on us.

Then his boss Horatio.

And finally, Maisie's mom Talia.

All of their sights set on the time machine gloved that glowed on the table, ready to take us home.

But it was too late.

Chapter Thirty-Four

"Looks like you're in a pickle, as you Americans say," Alexi said, pointing the gun. We all raised our hands into the air. "Which makes little sense because you are implying a pickle is bad, when in Russia we pickle everything."

Horatio made a move for the glove. "And thank you for removing my biggest competition in Scoot. We threw the body in the furnace so no one will ever know. Easier than tricking him out of the company."

Alexi swiveled the gun over to me. "The bullet was meant for Miles."

Horatio gave a smug smile. "You all will be meeting your end soon anyway." He picked up the glove, drooling. "I've waited for this for a long time."

Maisie turned to Talia. "And you're okay with them killing me...Mom?"

Talia seemed flummoxed. "Mom?"

Maisie blew out her cheeks. "I'm your daughter. Duh, from the future."

"I...I..." Talia couldn't finish her thought. She looked to Horatio for an explanation.

Maisie thrust her finger at Horatio. "He will send you back in time and you will disappear. No one knows what era you wind up in, but you leave me. And you were a good mom. Unless that was all fake?"

"I..." Talia's eyes shifted into machine mode. "I do this for the cause."

"And what's the cause?" I ask.

Still reeling from what she heard, Talia could barely speak. "To...enrich the future by fixing the past."

Horatio mouthed those words as well, obviously a tenet at Nimo.

"Then how do you explain working for Russia?" Maisie asked.

Talia took a beat to formulate her thoughts. "You think America is such a good country? We are responsible for genocide."

Maisie couldn't even look at her. "And Russia isn't?"

"This is moot," Horatio said. "We were partnering with Russia to get the parts for our own machine. You don't understand how expensive they can be."

Simon shook his head. "I managed to create a machine without the help from a foreign adversary."

Horatio petted the glove. "Yes, and now that we have the machine, we don't need the adversary anymore."

Talia seemed like she wanted to chew him to pieces. "What?"

"Talia," Horatio said, putting on his smooth tone. I could see how he got his underlings to follow. "Don't you see? You don't need to be a go-between anymore. I will pay you infinitely more just working for me. Not Nimo, for Nimo is dead. I've always enjoyed anagrams, so we will be born as Omni."

"Horatio, you told me this would assist in bridging the gap between the US and Russia," Talia said. "That together we could take over time."

He stroked her hair with his free hand. "My pet, we still can. Now that we have this glove, Russia will want to sink even more money into our project because there is always room for improvement." He turned to Simon. "Boy genius, you said this took you back twenty-five years in the past, right? And what were the side effects? Some prolonged bloody noses? But what if you tried to go back fifty years, a hundred, a thousand, the ice age? Would that be too much for our bodies to handle?"

"Yes, likely with that glove, we are not ready," Simon said. "You would be torn to a billion pieces in the tunnel before you'd arrive."

"But if Russia keeps pumping billions into research…" Horatio continued to pet Talia's hair, and I wondered if the two had a relationship. "You can still be our consigliore, Talia, if you want. Your role would be even more important."

Maisie stamped your foot. "This man will send you into the past and you'll never return. Is that what you want? To leave your family?"

"No…" she said. "I mean…you're not my family yet. I don't know you."

"But you will," Maisie said. "You'll be my mom. And I know you loved me. I have to know that."

I swiveled over to Alexi, who still trained the gun at us. "You're okay with your boss selling out Russia?"

Alexi laughed. "I am more than okay. Didn't I tell

you what my country did to my family? I owe them nothing. I owe him everything."

Horatio beamed. "That's a good soldier."

Maisie wiped away her flowing tears. "Don't you owe me anything, Mom?"

"Don't call me that," Talia hissed under her breath. She pulled away from Horatio, tapping her foot out of nervousness.

Maisie ran over. "They will kill me. Your only daughter. Do you want that blood on your hands?"

"You're lying." She glanced up at us all for support. "The girl is lying. I never wanted children, so there's no way…"

"But you had one," Maisie screamed. "You took on the responsibility, and you were good at it. If I was sick, you'd let me stay at home from school and we'd watch soap operas. You read me to sleep every night. You'd give me Eskimo kisses when I was feeling down. And I never knew you worked for this horrible company. You kept that from me because you thought you were doing good in this world or something…"

Talia tugged on her lip with her fang tooth. "I am doing good."

Maisie shook her head. "No, you're not. Whatever they told you, it's a lie."

"You're the lie."

"You told me a story about when you were little. Your parents had taken you on vacation and you rented a house. The owners were showing you around and you snuck away to slide down the banister. You were so excited. But broke it as you slid down. And then when the owners asked how it happened, you said the banister just fell off. Like that. They believed it. And you never told anyone. Except me. I was young and learned about secrets. Something happened at school and I didn't want to tell you. I was embarrassed. I wet myself and I thought my dad would be angry because I was too old to keep doing it. You let me tell you that secret and shared your own. You washed my pissy jeans, and we never spoke of it again."

Talia put her hand to her mouth, her eyes squeezing back tears. "I never told anyone that story."

"Until you had a daughter," Maisie said. "Who you loved more than anyone else."

"Enough!" Horatio snapped, causing us all to jump in place. "Start executing them, Alexi, and we will be off."

Maisie grabbed Talia's arm. "No, Mom, please… please don't do this."

Alexi went to fire the first bullet, lining his sights with Maisie. "Talia, step out of the way," he said.

Talia froze in place.

Horatio roared in her ear. "Talia, move away from the girl and you won't ever have to think about her again."

A lone tear trickled down Talia's cheek. "No," she said, so quietly I could barely hear.

"What was that?" Horatio thundered.

"No!" Talia screamed, stepping fully in front of Maisie who grinned out of relief.

"Fine," Alexi said. "I'll start with the boy genius."

I knew he wasn't talking about me.

Alexi trained the gun on Simon. I could see the wheels turning in Simon's brain trying to figure out how to get out of this pickle.

"That would be a negative," I heard from behind me, as Mr. Congley stood with the gun I'd obtained from Irma before she died. "Chekov's gun," he said as he fired a bullet that clipped Alexi in the skull.

Alexi went down fast. The blood oozed from his skull that cracked. He was deader than dead, and I felt a twinge in my heart because I had truly liked him. I was even infatuated when I thought he was someone else. I never expected this end for him, but he chose his dark path.

Chaos ensued as everyone started shouting and screaming. But I was focused on the glove. Horatio tucked it into his chest like a football and rushed toward the ladder.

"He's getting away," I said, running after him.

With one hand, Horatio flew up the ladder and burst out of the underground lab.

I followed behind, emerging from the earth.

I dug down deep to run faster.

I chased him to be able to go home, for if I didn't catch up, we'd never get to leave.

He was inches away as I leaped, my arms reaching out to tackle him to the ground.

Chapter Thirty-Five

We rolled around on the ground, kicking and clawing at each other. Both out for blood. Horatio was a demon in the way he fought, not human anymore. The gloved time machine was all that mattered. He snapped at me with his teeth, chewed flesh from my shoulder. I gripped him by the back of his head, smashed it into the ground. Blood spilled between us, no way to tell whose. He laughed like a madman through it all. I grabbed the glove and we wrestled as he held on tight, spun down a hill cut up by rocks and dirt.

"You will not keep me from my destiny," he roared.

"You won't keep me from mine," I yelled back.

He kicked me in the balls but I didn't give up. I fought harder. If we never returned to the present, Mom might have gotten better but she'd fall apart if both her sons vanished. It would destroy my parents, leaving them worse off than when we left. And who knows what Horatio would accomplish with the power of the glove? Giving it to Russia to make them more of a threat and building an even stronger machine, one that could even jump into the future. He could take over time completely and we'd all be at his bidding.

"No," I screamed in his face. "I won't let you win."

He let go of the glove, and for a second, I thought I was triumphant. But he'd shifted to wrap his fingers around my neck. Pressing down on my windpipe, I couldn't get air. My face turning purple. A wheeze passing from my lips. He gnashed his teeth, grinning like a psycho, enjoying taking my life.

I thought of all I'd done in my fifteen years. Not much until I saved my brother's life a few months ago. I'd refused to accept that Simon had taken his life and knew he'd been murdered. Traveling a week back in time, I used my detective skills to stop his killer. And I was successful. We'd gotten Maisie's evil dad thrown in jail. It was the greatest case that Mr. Hardy's Detective Agency ever had—until this one. Traveling back further to save Mom. And I did—I got her out of her abusive house. Hopefully stopped her from relying on pills to cope. Infiltrated Nimo and removed the threats of my grandfather and a spy. This was not how it was meant to end. Not on this hill with the life being squeezed out of me.

But I couldn't imagine letting go of the glove. I held on as if removing my hands meant a sure death. Horatio seemed surprised by my stubborn will. He'd likely assumed I'd have given up by now, but I gripped the glove tighter than ever as it glowed wildly, outlining us in a bluc orb.

Everything started to go hazy as I struggled for air.

This would be the end.

A sad tear dripped from my eye.

Horatio cackled at my defeat.

I felt the glove slipping from my hands.

And then it was gone, tumbling away. My heart scooped out of my chest too.

Horatio flipped me over until he was on top of me, at a better angle to choke me to death.

I flailed around, trying to grab the glove as he screeched above.

A gunshot rang out.

Horatio's eyes got wide as the back of his head exploded and he collapsed over me.

Simon stood in the distance with a smoking gun.

I screamed as I threw Horatio off of me. Got to my feet and checked to see my body was intact. Despite some scrapes and bruises, I was all right, after I hacked and vomited a bit until my breath came back.

"Get the glove," Simon said.

I picked up its glow and walked beside him.

"You saved my life," I said, my throat on fire.

He gave a tiny grin. "Only fair, since you saved mine our last trip. Now we're even."

I wrapped my arm around him and gave a strangling hug. "Brother for life."

He repeated back in our Okoboji language. "Brother for life."

Our hug-fest ended when we looked over at Horatio's dead, bloated body.

"He's not gonna be easy to carry up this hill, is he?"

Simon shook his head. "Far from it."

I stuffed the glove down my shirt and took Horatio's legs as Simon grabbed under his arms and we hoisted him up the hill. Once we got on steady ground, we dragged him the rest of the way, tossing him down the trapdoor along with the trail of bloody leaves we left behind. He landed in the lab with a thud and we climbed down to the surprise of Maisie, her mom, and Mr. Congley.

They all seemed to hold their breath until I whipped out the glowing glove and thrust it on the table.

"Party over, out of time," I shouted. "I've had enough of 1999."

Chapter Thirty-Six

Congley readied the glove as we all prepared to travel home. He promised to take care of Horatio and Alexi's dead bodies. Because of the clandestine work at Nimo, he doubted anyone would come looking for either of them. Then he and Simon said their goodbyes.

"I look forward to working with you again in twenty-five years," Congley said, reaching out his hand to shake.

Simon shook it heartily. "It'll only feel like a day for me, but I'm looking forward too. We couldn't have done this without you."

Congley waved a finger. "No, the student surpassed the teacher."

"I wouldn't have been able to create the glove if not for your mentorship."

"I'll make sure to look after your folks as well. Make sure Patty's doing all right in particular."

"Thanks," Simon said as Congley pulled him in for a hug.

Talia still seemed shell-shocked, so I went over to her.

"Are you all right?"

She shrugged. "My whole worldview has been turned upside-down."

"What's the expression?" I asked. "We can't see the forest for the trees."

"I was definitely blind."

Maisie walked over. "You meant to do good."

"I'm embarrassed," Talia said, putting her head in her hands.

"Nah, you're just still young," Maisie said.

"Wise words coming from…my teenage daughter. I still can't wrap my mind around that. What am I gonna do with my life?"

Maisie took her hand. "You're gonna meet my dad. And despite his faults…"

I gave Maisie a lingering look.

She nodded. "Despite his faults, he was good to you. And me. Maybe with you not being connected to Omni will keep him away from it too?"

"Why, what happens to him?" she asked.

I stepped between them. "It's not good to know too much about your future, right?"

Maisie put on a fake smile. "Right. We're happy for a lot of my childhood. And you're obviously passionate about whatever you put your mind to."

"Maybe you can work with Russia still, but in creating better relations between us and them," I said. "So you won't have to change your entire life plan."

Talia rubbed her head. "It's all overwhelming. And Horatio…" Her lip started to tremble.

Maisie took her hand again. "He was a bad man. But it's not your fault. He was obviously good at getting people to do what he wanted. Look at Simon's grandfather, or…" She gestured over to Alexi. "The other dead guy."

Congley called us. "Folks, it's time for you to go soon."

I stepped away. "I'm going to let you two say goodbye."

"Mom?" Maisie said.

"It'll still take me a while to get used to hearing that." Maisie shrugged. "But I'm glad I raised such a great young woman. Someone with ideals and convictions, like myself, but wiser."

Maisie hugged her. "It's all from you."

Talia inhaled a deep breath. "I believe that."

"You're strong," Maisie said. "You did what was right and saved all of us. Saved time."

Talia stood up straighter. "I did."

"Brilliantly," Maisie said, hugging her one last time. She let go and gave one more squeeze. "I love you, Mom."

Talia's words caught in her throat. "I love you too…daughter."

The glove began to glow more than before as Simon slipped it on his hand. He held onto me, and I touched Maisie. Lightning sparks showered the lab. A flash of blue nearly blinded us, and then we were gone.

We soared through the tunnel whirling by an explosion of colors. A vortex sucking us toward the present. Years flying by where I imagined visions of those I loved growing older. My parents building a life together. Talia finding her way without Horatio and Omni. Congley dedicating himself to teaching while he waited for Simon as a student.

Stars zoomed by as the universe reformed. We

grabbed each other's hands as we were thrust into the expanse. Hurling at such a speed that our faces morphed to glue. We turned into Picasso paintings, our body parts askew until the tunnel slowed down, collecting our broken pieces and putting us back together.

A circle pierced the universe and expanded. Growing wider and wider until we fit through, spitting us back out to the exact spot where we jumped.

As we rose to our feet on shaking knees, it had only been a few hours in time since we departed.

But it felt like a lifetime.

Chapter Thirty-Seven

Blood gushed out of our noses once we landed back in the present. Standing proved difficult. We flopped around like we had one too many, even though I'd never known what it was like to be drunk. Once we got our bearings and the blood stopped pouring, we checked to make sure we successfully jumped with all our parts intact. So far, the world looked the same. We hadn't reinvigorated the dinosaur age or anything like that with the changes we made. A plane sailed overhead. Birds chirped. A wild hare hopped along. We were home.

"I'm going to bring the glove down to the lab to keep it safe," Simon said, all business.

"You nervous?" I asked Maisie.

She was picking her cuticles. "I don't know if my mom will be there when I get home. Or my dad."

"Same here. We won't know until we know."

"I just want to give it a minute more. Until I find out."

"Me too."

It was awkward between us. We had made up but I didn't know if we were still together or not.

"Maisie, I…"

She held up her palm. "Miles, I think we should… what I'm trying to say…" She threw up her hands. "Ugh, I don't know what I'm trying to say."

"You want to be friends?"

She looked relieved. "Yes! I mean, I didn't want to sound so excited but—"

"It's a relief."

"Yes, yes, it is."

Even though this burned me to hear, I understood.

"We're so young still," she said. "And I think we both aren't sure yet what we want. And if I'm still at A.A. in Chicago, the distance makes it tough…"

I was trying not to cry. "I want you in my life."

"I do too," she said. "But I think for us to stay in each other's lives, it's better if we do it as friends."

I gestured to her nose. "You still have a little bit of blood."

"Maybe I'm keeping it for the memory."

Maisie kissed me on the cheek. "I couldn't ask for a better first relationship than you, Miles. Well, there has been a lot of drama, but it's gonna inspire me to paint some amazing things."

I sniffed back a tear. "I'm glad I could be a muse."

She sniffed back a tear too. "The best one. And you'll be a better muse as my friend, my best friend."

We held hands and let the moment sit with us for a minute until she let go and walked off.

"I'll text you when I get home," she called over her shoulder. "I hope your mom is all better too."

"So do I," I said as Simon climbed back up from the lab.

"Why are you crying?" he asked.

I wiped my sleeve around my eyes. "I'm not."

"Okay, Miles, whatever you say. So, you ready to go home and see how Mom's doing?"

I shook my head.

"C'mon," he said, his arm around my neck, dragging me forward.

When we got to our house, we stood outside. I didn't know what Simon was thinking, but I was afraid. I'd be crushed if everything we'd been through was for nothing. We had to have changed Mom. When I first traveled back in time, I saved Simon.

And this time…

The door swung open as we both held our breath.

Mom stood there, in a shirt and jeans that were clean, already a good first sign. Except for a dollop of flour by her collar.

"What are you two doing standing out here?" she asked. "I'm making cookies."

Both of us charged toward Mom and gave the biggest hug that almost knocked her down.

"What did I do to deserve this?" she asked, laughing. "You two never hug anymore now that you're both teenagers."

"Then we're overdue," I said, hugging her tighter.

"C'mon, c'mon," she said, waving us inside. "The cookies are gonna burn."

Stepping inside our home had a completely different energy. What once was sad and dark had been transformed. Mom's influence all over the walls with her artwork. Photographs of us as a family ascended up the stairs.

"Is that a Discman, Miles?" Mom asked. I had stuffed it in my pocket, but it was spilling out.

Shit, maybe she'd remember she gave it to someone named Alex so many years ago.

"Yeah," I said, stuffing it back down. "Retro is cool again."

"Hi, Miles," Dad said, walking up from the basement. He had more hair than I remembered him having and lost a few pounds from his midsection. He went over and kissed Mom on the cheek.

"How did the meeting go?" Mom asked.

"You mean the UniZoom Zoom meeting?" Dad said with a laugh.

"I bet it went…fast," Mom added, nudging him in the stomach.

"Well, we're not reinventing the wheel," he said, and the two of them laughed harder.

Simon and I caught each other's eye. It was rare to hear any laughter in our home. They seemed so in love still, rubbing each other's backs as tears crinkled from their eyes.

"I made oatmeal raisin," Mom said.

I could barely focus. "Wha…?"

The stove dinged. "Trying to be a little healthy here, so I used coconut sugar too."

I licked my lips. "That sounds amazing."

She stepped closer, her head slightly tilted. "I just had the strangest sense of déjà vu."

I gulped. "Oh yeah? What was it?"

"That's the thing about déjà vu. You know you can recall something, but just can't put your finger on exactly what. It's a nice feeling though, warm." She went to go to the kitchen, but stopped. "Your nose, Miles."

"Oh," I said, wiping away the blood fast. "I bumped it."

"C'mere." She whipped a tissue out of her sleeve, wet it with saliva, and dabbed the blood away. "Gotta be more careful."

"Thank you," I said, my heart full.

"Go on, get your grandma," she said. "She loves oatmeal raisin."

My stomach dropped. Which grandma did she mean? Could Grandma Ill still be alive? Or was it Grandma Denise?

I headed up the stairs, past photographs of the family from vacations I never went on. The Grand Canyon. Disneyworld. Even Europe! Part of me felt sad that this other Miles got to have such a wonderful childhood while I was shafted. But I couldn't stay upset. There'd be plenty more memories to make as a family. Even starting now.

I heard the sound of someone singing when I reached the top of the stairs. Peering into the bedroom, Grandma Denise sat on the bed crocheting a blanket. She was graying and heartier but still with big rosy cheeks.

"Oh Miles," she said when I entered. "How my favorite grandson doing?"

I was shell-shocked, barely able to speak.

"There's cookies downstairs," was all I could say. "Oatmeal raisin."

Chapter Thirty-Eight

"I love oatmeal raisin," Grandma Denise said, and put down her crochet. It seemed like altering with time had worked again! She must have listened to me by getting a mammogram and catching the cancer early. I was woozy and had to sit down. On the wall was a painting of a duck splashing around in a pond. I let it calm me until I could speak.

"I love oatmeal raisin too," I said, trying not to turn into a ball of mushy tears.

Grandma Denise laughed. "You look like you've seen a ghost."

I tried to laugh along.

"Boo!" she said, and I jumped.

Grandma Denise eyed the open door. She rose from the bed and went over to close it before sitting back down. The air felt thick, and my palms got sweaty.

"Did you return?" she asked, very serious.

My stomach rumbled out of nervousness. "What do you mean?"

"Miles," she said, chiding. She shook her finger. "I know."

I scraped my teeth together. "Know what?"

She dropped her voice to a low hum. "Time…"

My eyes bugged as I leaped out of the chair.

"No, no, Miles, it's okay. Oh, sweetie, I've scared you."

"How do you…know?"

She patted the bed. "Come, sit by me."

I was hesitant, unable to trust anyone. Could she be working for Omni? My brain couldn't keep up with my conspiracies.

"Oh, come now." She patted the bed again, so I went over.

As I sat, she rubbed my back. I had to admit it felt good.

"I know Simon invented a time machine." Her cheeks reddened as she put a finger to her lips. "Your mother and father don't know, but I was always suspicious. A couple of years ago, you started to look like someone I'd met I long time ago. A boy named Miles. Your parents knew of him as Alex, but you told me who you really were."

I struggled to swallow, completely clueless as to where this was headed.

Grandma Denise clapped her hands. "How could I forget? You saved my life. This curious boy who told me to get a mammogram. And I almost didn't listen. I was lying in bed one night and couldn't stop thinking of why you would tell me that. So, I booked an appointment the next day and sure enough…cancer. But we caught it so early. It was a harder road in 1999 than it would be now, since it was Stage 2 but not aggressive. In another six months, I wouldn't have stood a chance. So, I've always thought about you. I would ask Kip and Patty about you, but they never heard from you or your brother again, speaking of you as Alex. Something made me not correct them. As if I knew I shouldn't reveal who you really were, an angel sent down to save me, oh that's how I looked at it then. But I never forgot you, Miles. When Kip and Patty named you Miles, well, deep inside, I had a feeling that something magical had occurred. And then, you grew up to look just like this angel who saved me."

She held on to my face, her eyes welling. "Simon was always working on a secret invention, and I had a sense that it had to do with you saving me twenty-five years ago. So, I confronted him, and he confessed. I promised never to tell anyone until the right time when I believed you needed to hear. The way you looked at me when you walked in just now…you've just come back, haven't you?"

I nodded as she drew me into her bosom for an engulfing hug.

"Thank you, Miles. Sweet Miles. I've been living on borrowed time, but it's wonderful. Truly. I've seen my children grow up and my grandchildren too."

"Your…children?"

She slapped her forehead. "Oh, right. I adopted Patty. Rather sad, but her mother passed after she came to stay with me. Drank herself right to death one night and her husband, your grandfather, had vanished, never to be heard from again. So, she became my daughter. And after college, her and Kip married and soon had Simon and then you. All because of you."

"Wow," I said. "That's what I hoped could happen, but I never thought…"

"Time moves in mysterious ways," Grandma Denise said. "Sometimes out of our favor, and other times, bends to our will."

Grandma Denise squeezed me again and then got up.

"Let's go get those cookies while they're hot. I would bet you've worked up an appetite." She pinched my cheek, opened the door, and waddled outside.

I was about to follow when my phone beeped. It hadn't worked at all in the past, but now was beeping up a storm. Texts from Maisie.

> Miles!

> How did it go w yer Mom? Hope she is OK.

> Mine is here! And she's wonderful. Just as I remembered.

> Not my dad. He's still in prison. Not for trying to kill your brother, but insider trading, whatever that is.

> I guess you can't fix a criminal.

> But I'm happy. Really happy.

> And I owe it to you, best friend.

> My true best friend.

She ended the text with a smiley face 😊
And I replied with the same 😊

Chapter Thirty-Nine

A few months later, I became a sophomore. The summer had been pretty cool. I hung out with Kevin a lot, really missing him and his goofiness. We updated our detective website and didn't have any dangerous cases, but that was okay with me. Mostly missing cats and that kind of thing, usually paid in pies. I wanted to spend time with Mom and Grandma Denise, so I hung around the house a lot. Mom and I would bake. Grandma Denise taught me crocheting, and I even made a blanket in the shape of a pizza. Dad took me around in his UniZoom that was getting heavy interest from investors. Once he sold, he promised us all another trip to Europe (well, a first one for me). We were thinking Ireland, and I was psyched to see the Cliffs of Moher and maybe try a Guinness beer.

Simon got into MIT and left for Boston, so it was weird not having him around. He was so busy over the summer with reading lists he had to do even before school started that often his door was closed. But right before he left, he knocked on mine one early morning and we took a walk to the underground lab. He was going to put the time machine glove away for a while and focus on new projects. We climbed down and opened a safe he built for the glove. Watching it glow one last time was bittersweet.

"We've changed the world," I said, but Simon just shrugged.

He slid his glasses up his nose. "I don't know if we've changed the world. But we've definitely changed our world."

"What are you talking about? Omni doesn't exist anymore."

He held up a finger. "That we know of…"

"Ugh," I said, feeling faint. "Don't freak me out."

"Okay, as of now, you don't have to worry." And then under his breath. "I'll do all the worrying."

"Simon!"

Simon laughed, a rare occurrence. "I'm just messing with you, Miles. Yes, Omni is gone."

He whipped out a raspberry scone. "From Irma's Bakery."

Irma had followed in her dream of opening a bakeshop in Frontier, far from working for Omni and trying to control time. She was the last relic left from the company besides Maisie's mom, who now worked as our government's ambassador to Russia.

Irma made really great raspberry scones. I gobbled one up.

"So, you gonna work on a new time machine up in Boston?" I asked him, licking the raspberry jam off my fingers.

He shook his head. "Nah, I don't want to be a one-trick pony. Let me invent something I can actually share with the scientific community. AI that could cure diseases, fix world hunger. That kind of thing."

"Safer than time," I said to him in Okoboji.

He replied in our secret language as well. "Safer than time."

"I gonna miss you, Simon," I said. "It's crazy because we used to hate each other—"

"Oh, I still hate you."

I punched him in the arm. "Shut up, no you don't."

"No, I really don't. I lucked out in the brother department."

"Brother for life," I said.

"Brother for life."

We shut the safe door on the glove, glowing no more.

"So, how's Maisie?" he asked. "You two still in touch?"

"Yeah, we are. As friends. But it's all good. She has a show in Chicago next weekend."

"Are you going to go?"

"I don't know. I mean, I don't really fit in with her art friends."

"So what? I'd bet she'd be glad to have you there. Maybe Mom could take you? It'll help her get over the fact that I'll be gone."

"Oh, she's already having a hard time. The number of pictures I've had to see of you over the last few weeks…"

"Go, and even bring Kevin. He could use leaving Frontier to expand his horizons."

I made a screwy face. "Since when do you care about Kevin?"

"I don't. But you do."

A week later, Mom was driving me and Kevin down to Chicago where we were all going to get a hotel for the night. Maisie didn't know, I was gonna surprise her. Kevin and I played punch buggy, since Mom wasn't a fan of phones in the car.

"Punch buggy red," Kevin said, whapping me in the arm as he ate from a bag of M&M's.

Twenty miles later, I punched his arm. "Punch buggy blue."

Mom turned on the radio and "Freak of the Week" by Marvelous 3 came on.

"I love this song," she said, turning it up. But I stayed quiet. That was the CD she gave me back in 1999, and I was always nervous she might remember. But she was lost in the song, singing as we entered Chicago.

The A.A. students were having a show at a gallery in Wicker Park. After we checked into the hotel, Mom dropped Kevin and me off at the gallery while she went to explore around town.

"I haven't been to Chicago in years," she gushed. "You call me when it's done."

"I will," I said as she gave me a kiss on the cheek.

I was still getting used to this excited Mom, but now I couldn't imagine her anyway else.

"Where's my kiss, Mrs. Hardy?" Kevin asked, holding out his freckled cheek.

Kevin admitted to having a crush on my mom. I hadn't told him about our trip back to 1999. He had a big mouth and it was just easier to accept our new reality as fact without worrying he'd spill our secrets.

Mom put her hand on her hip. "All right, Kevin."

She kissed him on the cheek as he pumped a fist into the air that made her laugh.

"Bye, boys. Be safe."

When we entered the gallery, I saw those two pretentious nitwits, Slade and Agatha, who had made fun of Maisie's art the last time. Slade wore what looked like a parachute and Agatha colored her hair silver like the Tin Man.

They walked over with their noses in the air.

"Maisie's friend…right?" they asked, about to devolve into a fit of laughter.

I puffed out my chest. "Yeah, her best friend."

Kevin stamped his foot. "Hey, I thought I was your best friend."

"Simpletons," I heard Agatha say and Slade agreed.

"Where's your art?" I asked.

Agatha gestured over to the wall where I saw a few oranges laid out, all sliced different ways.

"It's a statement on farmability and our dwindling resources."

Kevin gave a thumbs down. "Looks like lunch to me."

Agatha bristled. "It's intellectually superior."

"Or just not really art," I said.

"That's me," Slade boasted and showed us a toilet seat. "It's a comment about our society being flushed down the toilet."

"It looks like you just bought a toilet," I said.

"Again, it's intellectually superior," Slade said as Maisie came over.

"Miles!" she shouted. Her hair was a billion colors, and she wore a sweater with a ton of holes in it and super baggy jeans. She looked cooler than I ever would be. "You came!" She saw Kevin. "You and Kevin."

Kevin gave a wave. "Hi, Maisie."

Maisie kissed me on the cheek and stroked my arm. "I'm so glad you're here. It really means a lot."

"I had to see your new art," I said. "As a best friend's muse."

Maisie put her hand to her heart. "I'm touched."

Agatha butted in. "They weren't understanding our work."

Maisie whispered in my ear. "Because no one does."

I grinned. "Where's your paintings?"

"Over there." Maisie pointed to a crowd. When Slade and Agatha looked over, I could see they were upset not to have the same kind of gathering.

We left them and Maisie parted the crowd to her work. So many people were commenting on how much they loved it, including a girl our age with a shaved head and blue lipstick.

"Miles, this is Gwenyth," Maisie said. "My... girlfriend."

A few months ago, I would've gone nuclear to hear that Maisie moved on, especially because I hadn't— well, I wasn't ready yet after what we all went through in the past. To be honest, I was more concerned on focusing on my family.

Gwenyth shook my hand. "I've heard so much about you. Maisie said the nicest things." She pointed at the wall. "You were her inspiration."

I stared at the paintings that everyone oohed and ahhed over. They told a story of our journeys. Flying through the tunnel. Straddling time and worlds. Saving moms from vortexes primed to suck them into oblivion. No one would be able to tell exactly what the paintings were about, but I understood. Especially the one of two silhouettes I imagined was me and Maisie, holding hands between the past and the present with the quote: "Time goes, you say? Ah, no! alas, time stays, we go."

I gave Maisie a side hug. "They're incredible. I'm so proud of you."

She whispered in my ear. "I'm so proud of us."

Afterward, we went to Franks N' Dawgs for porkgasms with ham dust and jalapeños. The four of us sat a booth, me and Kevin, Maisie and her girlfriend Gwenyth. We devoured our hot dogs and got a sugar high from their big sodas. I liked Gwenyth. She was quiet but very sweet, and I could see she adored Maisie. They held hands throughout lunch and shared bites with one another while Kevin told inappropriate jokes and we all laughed. I'd catch Maisie's eye every once in a while, and she'd wink. Every time, she did, I couldn't help but smile.

We were about to leave when "Closing Time" by Semisonic came on the radio.

Maisie jumped out of her seat, ordering the guy behind the counter to turn it up.

The song blasted as we started to sing along, both Kevin and Gwenyth flummoxed, since they didn't know the song at all.

But Maisie and I didn't care. We danced and danced, flinging our arms and not caring who was watching. We had traveled in a way that no one ever had before and returned better from our journeys, fixing our families, fixing each other.

We shouted out the chorus at the top of our lungs, arm-in-arm, like the best of friends for life, singing until our throats were sore.

Every new beginning comes from some other beginning's end...

A Look At Runaway Train: The Complete YA Contemporary Coming-Of-Age Trilogy

An Epic Journey of 90s Teenage Rebellion

In "Runaway Train," set against the backdrop of the grunge music scene and fueled by the spirit of Kurt Cobain and rage after her sister's tragic death, 16-year-old Nico Sullivan decides to break free from her troubles. Armed with her bucket list and a mixtape of 90s hits, she sets off on a cross-country adventure, seeking solace and self-discovery. Along the way, she encounters a series of unexpected twists and turns that will leave you both laughing and shedding tears.

"Grenade Bouquets" catapults Nico into the spotlight as she chases her dreams of becoming a rockstar. Her journey takes her on a rollercoaster ride through the music industry, love, and personal growth. As she grapples with fame, substance abuse, and the ghosts of her past, Nico's resilience shines through, making this novel a powerful testament to the transformative power of music and self-belief.

In the final installment, "Vanish Me," Love, Nico's estranged daughter, embarks on a quest to find her missing mother. With every page of Nico's old diary as a guide, Love, accompanied by her friends Frankie and Caden, delves into the enigmatic world of her mother's past. Along the way, she discovers a shared love for 90s grunge music and learns to confront her own insecurities and abandonment issues.

Get ready to dive into a world of teenage rebellion, music, and self-discovery as you follow Nico and Love's journeys through the pages of this captivating trilogy. Don't miss out on this epic saga of love, loss, and the indomitable spirit of youth.

AVAILABLE NOW

About the Author

Lee Matthew Goldberg is the author of the novels THE ANCESTOR, THE MENTOR, THE DESIRE CARD, SLOW DOWN and ORANGE CITY. He has been published in multiple languages and nominated for the 2018 Prix du Polar. After graduating with an MFA from the New School, his writing has also appeared in The Millions, Vol. 1 Brooklyn, LitReactor, Monkeybicycle, Fiction Writers Review, Cagibi, Necessary Fiction, the anthology Dirty Boulevard, The Montreal Review, The Adirondack Review, The New Plains Review, Underwood Press and others.

He is the editor-in-chief and co-founder of Fringe, dedicated to publishing fiction that's outside-of-the-box. His pilots and screenplays have been finalists in Script Pipeline, Book Pipeline, Stage 32, We Screenplay, the New York Screenplay, Screencraft, and the Hollywood Screenplay contests. He is the co-curator of The Guerrilla Lit Reading Series and lives in New York City. RUNAWAY TRAIN and its sequel GRENADE BOUQUETS will be his first Young Adult novels from Wise Wolf Books in 2021.

Follow him at LeeMatthewGoldberg.com